THEIR PROMISE

HER ROYAL HAREM: LILY
BOOK ONE

CATHERINE BANKS

TURBO KITTEN INDUSTRIES

To Avery for his support and love.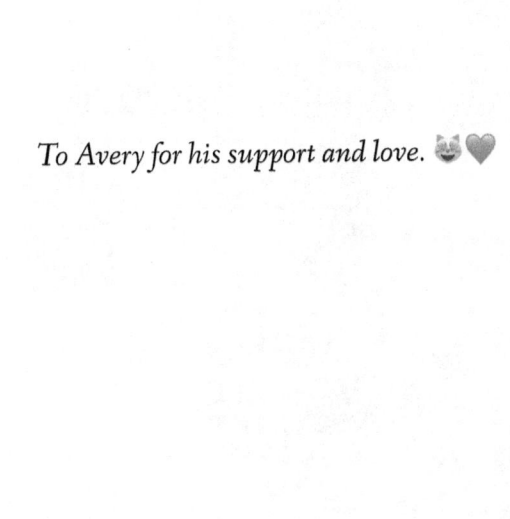

CHAPTER
ONE

I had been away from my pack and family for six consecutive months. A total of six years, on and off. Now, I was finally finished with my degree and heading home. I anxiously watched the scenery through the train's window, wondering what my friends and family were doing. My phone was suspiciously quiet, something very unusual in my life. The train came to a smooth stop and everyone in the car stood to grab their bags, myself included. My large suitcase was in the back and I would get it after exiting the train.

Hiking my backpack up higher, I walked out of the train car and searched for whoever was picking me up. I assumed it would be one of my parents or my childhood guard, Ezio.

As I surveyed the area, I realized I didn't see any of them. Heading towards the rear of the train where my luggage was, pain filled my chest that they could have forgotten about me. The pain burned hot as it morphed into rage.

Deep within me was a stirring pit of boiling anger, caused by a personality alteration spell I had absorbed to save my adoptive mother when I was five years old. Most of the time I was able to keep it contained with little effort, but some emotions, like sadness, allowed it to stir.

My purple and cyan streaked hair started to glow softly from the awakening of the anger and darkness in my soul. Stopping, I closed my eyes, took a deep breath, and reminded myself of my loving family, my best female friend Maya, and my grandparents and great grandparents who cared deeply for me. I was not alone. I was loved. I was happy. The magic and anger were not me and would not control me.

Successfully calmed, I opened my eyes and resumed walking, a skip in my step as I moved. I knew my parents remembered I was coming; Mom had messaged me several times this morning to make sure I didn't forget anything and was ready. They were probably just running late, as per usual. When your parents were king and queen of a clan, they quite frequently got called to emergencies. It was something I had become accustomed to.

The man unpacking the luggage saw me and bowed. "Your Highness, your luggage is right here." He wheeled over my large, bright pink suitcase with an adorable bunny on the side that reminded me of Mom's animal form. "Do you need me to call a car or anything?" he asked, looking around me and seeing I was alone.

"That won't be necessary," a deep, familiar voice said behind me.

Spinning around, mouth open in a wide smile, I threw my arms around Ezio's neck. "You didn't forget me!"

He chuckled as he hugged me and patted the back of my head. "Silly girl. I could never forget you." Ezio was getting older. Grey lined his temples that hadn't been there when I first met him as a child, and his forehead creases were deepening, which he blamed on me giving him extra stress. He was one of the strongest werewolf alphas, but his age was starting to catch up with him. When I was a child, he had been my guard, protecting me from harm and helping to teach me how to behave in shifter society. "Just this one suitcase?" he asked as he grabbed the handle.

I nodded. "Grandpa Nico teleported the rest of it last week when they came for my graduation ceremony." Grandpa Nico was King of the Mages and the most powerful mage in the world. He was kind and one of the most sarcastic males in my family, next to Caleb, my adoptive father, of course.

Ezio shook his head. "I don't understand why they had you ride the train when your mother or Nico could teleport you back."

"I asked to ride the train," I explained and looped my arm through his. "I wanted the full college experience, but Grandpa Nico convinced me that trying to drag four additional suitcases would ruin the positive experience and left me with the one."

Chuckling, Ezio looped his arm around my shoulders and squeezed. "I've missed you, kid."

Resting my head against his shoulder I admitted, "I missed you, too. How's Holly?"

Holly was Ezio's wife, one of several hybrids we had discovered on an island that had been thought to be uninhabited when I was young, and who had come to live with our clan. She was sweet, powerful, and when angry, a bit scary.

Since Ezio was like an uncle to me, I'd spent a lot of time at their house and she'd treated me just like a second child. That included a few spankings when her son, Kayden, and I had gotten into trouble together.

Thinking about Kayden made my chest ache. We had been friends growing up, but he had said something that hurt me so much I stopped talking to him about four years ago. That was about the same time our mutual best friend, Trey, had stopped talking to me as well. Probably a boy solidarity pact or something. Thoughts of them had that darkness and anger swirling.

"Are you excited to be done with college?" Ezio asked. He glanced at my hair that had started glowing and frowned, knowing my darkness was awakened if it glowed.

"Yes. It'll be nice to be home and reacquaint myself with the clan and spend more time with my parents," I said. My life had been spent surrounded by people who loved me and ensured I never wanted for anything. Going away to college had been a big change, but one I had desperately needed.

We headed out to the street and I squealed and dashed away from Ezio when I saw Maya, my best female friend. "Maya!" I screamed.

She ran to me, crashing together as we hugged each other. "Lily!" she squealed.

We held each other in a bone crunching hug for several long minutes, just needing to be touching again after being apart for so long. I was careful not to hug too tightly, my animal side was a constrictor and if I wasn't careful, I could seriously hurt her.

Maya had been my first friend, one of the island hybrids,

and when she moved to our clan territory, we had been inseparable throughout our childhood until her parents had moved away and she'd gone with them. We had called and messaged each other every single day and ensured we saw each other for at least one holiday a year. Just a few months ago, she'd moved back to the city.

"We're finally together," I exhaled and leaned back to look at her. Her fiery red hair was curly and wild like usual, puffed around her face, framing it in what seemed like flames. Though, that wasn't far off, since she turned into a flaming bird.

"I've missed you so much," she said and hugged me again.

"Get in the car, girls. You can hug inside," Ezio ordered us.

"Yes, sir!" she said, released me, saluted him, and climbed inside.

Giggling at her over the top theatrics, I climbed into the backseat with her.

"So, did you meet any cute boys on the train?" Maya asked.

Ezio growled softly.

Chuckling, I shook my head. "Nope."

She groaned. "I'm supposed to live vicariously through you. How am I supposed to do that if you're not meeting any boys?"

"It's not like I control where they are," I reminded her. She knew I had started quietly looking for guys to date. Announcing that to my family would spell disaster for sure. "Besides, I'm sure we'll meet some guys at the club tomorrow."

She flinched. "About that ..."

"Oh, no. What?" I asked.

"Your great grandparents are all in town and they called for a party to celebrate everyone being together for the first time in like a decade," she said, her words so fast I barely understood them. "So, they're throwing this big shindig thing and we're supposed to dress up really nice and go to that big building where they have the fundraisers and stuff. I tried to get out of it, but Mom Two said it was mandatory."

Mom Two was what Maya called my mother, since she was like her second mother.

"You know the former royals haven't all been back at the same time in quite a while," Ezio said as he drove us towards our clan territory. "They've all missed you a lot and it'll mean the world to them if you go."

"It's totally fine," I said with a smile. "I haven't seen Great Grandpa Dan or Great Nana Kara in months, so it'll be nice. We can do the club another day."

Maya squealed again. "I'm honestly excited for tomorrow. Mom Two said she's going to have all of your favorite foods, which means lots of sweets, too! I hope she remembers the lemon bars."

"Those are your favorite," I reminded her with a soft laugh and shake of my head.

"Oh, right," she said.

Ezio laughed at us, smiling wide. "I've missed you two rambunctious girls. It's been far too quiet without you running around the clan territory."

I wanted to ask about Kayden, but my pride had me keeping my mouth shut on the topic in case he told Kayden I had asked about him, since I didn't want him to know I cared still.

"Do you know what your plan is after your break?" Maya asked.

I'd asked my parents to give me a month break after I finished college before sucking me back into royal duties, and they'd agreed without much hesitation. I knew after that one month was up, all bets were off though.

"I'll have to start pulling my weight as princess," I answered. "I'm sure they'll have me take over one of the businesses now that I have a degree in business administration." Part of the reason I'd opted to go to college was to increase my knowledge to help our clan. We were much smaller in number of members than the others, so it was important that we did all we could to ensure we were monetarily safe.

A thought occurred to me. "Wait, we're having a party tomorrow when we're already having a party for my birthday next week?"

Ezio said, "Your birthday party won't include all the cousins and distant relatives. So, they opted for a party tomorrow to include everyone."

"Everyone?" I asked softly.

Maya put her hand on top of mine on my lap, sensing my unease.

Ezio arched a brow. "Is there someone you have a problem with that you don't want to see? Did something happen between you and one of the others?"

If I admitted it was Kayden, he would ask me a billion questions since he was his son. So, instead, I just shook my head and said, "No, just thinking about how many people that will be and how I'm going to get bombarded since I've been away for so long." The distant family hadn't seen me since I started college six years ago, so they would definitely swamp me with questions.

Ezio didn't look convinced, but he focused on the road again. "Do you want me as a guard?"

"Ezio, I'm an adult now. I can handle the party. I just know I'm going to get bombarded is all."

"The offer stands. Remember, everyone had guards during the turbulent times in their adult lives, even your father and mother." He gave me a look. "So, don't you, 'I'm an adult now,' me, missy."

Laughing, I said, "Thanks, Ezio. I'll keep it in mind if I do end up needing a rescue."

"I'll be at the party," he said, "so don't hesitate to yell for me."

But would he rescue me from his own son?

TWO

"My girl!" Mom shouted as she ran out of the house and tackle hugged me, sending us rolling across the grass.

Laughing, I squeezed her and nuzzled my nose into her neck to inhale her scent. "Hi, Mama."

"I missed you," she whined as she hugged me.

"Stop strangling our daughter," Dad said and pulled her off of me, only for him to immediately scoop me up under the armpits and crush me against his chest in his own hug. "Hello, Lily."

"Hello, Caleb."

He growled, hating when I used his name.

"Where are my other fathers?" I asked. Mom was Queen of the Hybrids and had four mates, including Caleb who was King of the Hybrids. Having so many dads made referring to them difficult, so most times I had to use their first names as well. Her other mates were Riddick, Branson, and Triston, all hybrid shifters. Caleb was the only one I called dad, though. When I'd gotten older, I'd asked them if it bothered them that

I only called Caleb dad, but they all swore it didn't bother them and they liked the nicknames I gave them.

"Your other fathers are busy with preparations for the party your grandparents decided to throw together last minute," he answered as he released me.

"Yes, Ezio informed me about it," I said and turned to see him carrying my suitcase up to the porch. "Ezio! Let me do that."

He growled at me. "Don't start with me. I can still throw a car with ease. I'm not *that* old."

Dad snickered. "He'll get a lot of that treatment from Kayden soon enough."

"Soon enough?" I asked, my heart starting to beat faster and my hair shimmering a bit.

"You think your best friend would miss your birthday?" Ezio asked with a scoff and shook his head.

"I'm her best friend," Maya countered as she walked over to me, putting her arm around my shoulders. "Kayden lost his chance –"

I elbowed her stomach, making her stop talking to grunt an exhale.

"Something happen between you two that I should know about?" Ezio asked.

Dad folded his arms across his chest and Mom stood from the grass, eyes wide.

Shit.

"No," I said quickly. "It's just been a few years since we've seen each other, so –"

"Years?" Ezio asked, scowling so hard his forehead wrinkles deepened. "You didn't see each other at Christmas?"

"Uh, no, um, we happened to miss each other," I lied. I had purposefully hidden and avoided him the three days I had been home.

"Come on, I'll help you unpack," Maya said, grabbed my hand, and dragged me and my suitcase inside.

When we got into my room with the door closed behind us, I exhaled in relief. "Thanks."

"Well, it was sort of my fault they started badgering you, sorry." She winced. "I know it's been hard to keep all that a secret from them."

Flopping down onto my bed, I shrugged and said, "It was bound to come out eventually."

She tossed the suitcase onto my bed, forcing me to roll off with a yelp to avoid getting hit by it. "Let's get you unpacked."

"What news is there since I left?" I asked as I unzipped the suitcase.

"The demon attacks are continuing to increase," she said as she threw the clothes from the suitcase into my hamper. "From what I've heard, Kayden, Trey, and Mason have been traveling around the various continents to help out where the most demon attacks are happening."

Kayden, Trey, and Mason were strong alphas and their dads ensured they were epically trained fighters, so it made sense to send them out to fight the demons. It did not do my heart and anxiety good to hear that, but I also knew it was necessary.

"What new couples are there?" I asked, knowing Maya loved gossiping about relationships and wanting to steer the topic away from the trio of males.

"Actually, none, it's been a pretty boring spring. I've been trying to set Jaeden up, but he just tells me he is too busy with his games. Nana Jolie is helping him and apparently testing out his game for him." She sighed dramatically. "I know the games are his obsession, but he needs someone to date, too. He can't just end up alone."

I hid my smirk from her, not wanting to have the same conversation about her liking him and not wanting to admit it. Jaeden was a sheep shifter, a bit timid, and every time he was around Maya, they orbited around each other without technically interacting. It was hilarious and Mom and I would huddle together to laugh about it. Someday, I was sure they'd admit their feelings and get together, but in the meantime, we ignored the topic.

"What about Ezra and Tomlin?" I asked. She'd been talking about them a few months ago.

She blew a raspberry. "Epic failure. They flirted a bit, but then stopped talking completely."

"No other rumors floating around?" I asked.

"Nope," she said, making the p sound pop. "So, boring."

"Well, I'm back now so I can help entertain you," I said.

"Right, how long until you start getting set up on blind dates?" she asked with a smile. "I know Mom was teasing you about that when you came back for Christmas."

I flinched. She had threatened, but I was fairly certain she wasn't serious. Mom hadn't found her mates until she was almost thirty, so I didn't think she was actually worried about me as I was only twenty-four, twenty-five in a week.

"Hopefully, that won't be necessary," I muttered.

Maya laughed and shook her head.

A dark envelope on my desk caught my eye. Who would have sent me such a fancy envelope? I stood to head towards my desk.

"Dinner!" Mom yelled from downstairs.

"Coming!" Maya and I called back. The envelope would have to wait.

"Do you have a dress picked out for tomorrow?" I asked.

She shook her head. "Mom Two said we could go shopping tomorrow morning for one together."

"Perfect," I said, and rolled my now empty suitcase into my closet before we jogged downstairs and to the dining room.

All of my fathers were back and they took turns hugging me and telling me how much they missed me. Branson, who I called Bran Bran, my bear shifter father, hugged me the tightest and longest. He and I had been the closest after I came to live with them and was raised by them, and he was also the one that could withstand my hugs the most.

We sat down at the table and I threw my head back as I laughed at the sight of chicken nuggets on the table. It had been my favorite thing when I first came here at four years old.

"Welcome home, Lily," Mom said and smiled wide. "We've missed you, and while we are so proud of you and the degree you've earned, we are very happy to have you back home with us. Now, let's eat and play some games!"

Being surrounded by the chatter and warmth of so many of my family eased the hole that had been growing while I was away. While I was a snake, which was a solitary creature, I as a hybrid shifter craved being surrounded by my pack.

The darkness within me became more suppressed and I breathed the first full breath in months.

"No, RED IS NOT YOUR COLOR," Maya said and shook her head at the dress I was trying on. "That style is cute, but not that color."

"I think I preferred the previous style on you better," Mom said and canted her head as she watched me turn in a circle. "Up to you, sweetheart."

"What about the previous style in that color?" I asked and pointed towards a nearby dress.

Maya and Mom both nodded and shouted simultaneously, "Yes!"

Finally finished with our dress purchases, we stopped at our favorite restaurant, Brickhouse, happening to find my Great Aunt Leona and one of her mates, Prince Silverowl of the Elves, eating.

"Hey!" she shouted and rushed over to hug me. "I'm so glad you're home!" She pushed me back, set a hand on my chest, closed her eyes, and after a moment smiled. "That darkness is wrapped up nice a tight. Well done, girl!"

Preening at her praise, I admitted, "It helped coming home."

Great Uncle Silverowl hugged me and tapped the middle of my forehead. "Your snake wants out. I can feel it." He had come over at least once a week to train with my fathers and subsequently, we had spent a lot of time training together as well. "When's the last time you shifted?"

"Snakes aren't exactly people's favorite animal," I reminded him. "Pretty sure the girls in my dorm would have burned the building to the ground if they'd seen me."

"Are you bigger?" Great Aunt Leona asked.

I nodded. "Yeah, a lot."

"Define a lot," Great Uncle Silverowl said with a frown.

"Come over after we eat and she can show you," Mom said. "We need to eat."

"Oh, were you shopping?" Great Aunt Leona asked and waved at the server, Tim, who immediately rushed over and added the empty table next to theirs to make a combined larger table so we could sit with them. One of the perks of being royalty was having people make accommodations for you that they wouldn't normally for others. I tried to avoid doing it because I felt bad to inconvenience people, especially since I'd been adopted into the family.

"Yes, buying dresses for tonight," Mom answered and sat. "Tim, can we get four of that sparkling wine that I like and our usuals?"

Tim was always our server when we came to this restaurant, so he was used to our requests. "Of course, Your Majesty. Are we still not eating onions?" he asked and looked at me.

My face scrunched as I said, "Of course I'm not eating onions still. They're gross."

Everyone laughed, including Tim.

He winked. "Just checking, Your Highness."

Mocking him silently as he walked away, I sat between

Mom and Great Aunt Leona and leaned my head on her shoulder. "I've missed you, Great Auntie."

She leaned her head over to rest atop mine. "I didn't miss you reminding me of my age."

Chuckling, I said, "Well, it has been about twenty years since I came into your lives."

"Ouch, way to make us feel old," Mom said and sighed. "I'm no longer part of the youngest generation of shifter adults."

Great Uncle Silverowl chuckled. "You don't look a day over twenty-five, Rubyhare."

Rubyhare was Mom's elven name, a descriptor of her animal form, a white rabbit with red eyes.

She smiled and said, "You're lucky, Leona. Any way you could train your nephew a bit better?"

I rolled my eyes. "Dad is super sweet to you."

"There's always room for improvement," Great Aunt Leona said as she shook her fork at me.

"I'll keep that in mind," I said.

"Speaking of that," Great Aunt Leona said in a higher pitched voice, "any prospects on the horizon?"

I scoffed and shook my head. "You're as bad as Maya."

"Hey!" Maya said with a hand to her chest.

"She's got time," Great Uncle Silverowl said softly. "You two mated ladies didn't find your mates until you were older than she is currently."

Tim returned with our glasses of sparkling wine, giving me time to take a sip before responding.

"If you want grandbabies, go bother my brother," I told Mom. "He should have even more prospects than me."

Maya scowled and took a large drink of hers.

Busted! She did have a thing for my brother. I knew it!

"He's much like your father," Mom said and shook her head. "Completely ignoring women, which I hope means he has a fated mate out there somewhere."

Maya's scowl turned into a frown of sadness. Oh, boy. She liked him even more than the last time we'd discussed him. Interesting.

"So, what time does the party start tonight? Will I have time for a shower?" I asked to change the subject.

"We're going to finish eating here and then head home so you can shower and change," Mom answered.

Tim brought out our food, and we ate the delicious chicken pasta and got one more drink before saying bye to Great Aunt Leona and Great Uncle Silverowl, and teleporting back home.

I hurried upstairs to shower, but the envelope I'd forgotten about last night caught my attention again. Walking over to it, I examined the black envelope with no return address listed. Opening it, I pulled out a card, my eyes widening at the letter's contents.

> Dear, Princess Liliana Rubyserpent of the
> Hybrids.
>
> Although communications have been sparse as
> there seems to be an issue with our phones, the
> upcoming date has necessitated that we correspond
> by letter. Our sworn promise is now at the time of
> enactment. I hope you remember the promise, but if

you have forgotten, we promised that if both sides are unmated upon your twenty-fifth birthday, we shall become mates. Although the promise was made when we were younger, it is still binding and as such, we will return to enact said promise. See you at the party, Princess.

Your friends,

Kayden, Trey, & Mason

Dropping the letter like it was on fire, my heart beat so wildly that I could hear it in my skull. My breathing became ragged and I slid to my knees, the darkness swirling within me quickly. My hair cast rainbows around the room forcing me to close my eyes against the brightness.

Yes, we had made a promise when we were kids, but that was it, a promise between kids! They couldn't seriously think that I would follow through with that silly promise now. Especially not after what had happened between us!

"We have to leave in thirty minutes!" Mom shouted from downstairs. "Hurry up, Lily!"

Taking a deep breath, I thought about it logically. They were all grown adults, warriors who fought and killed demons to protect the world, and had lived away from their parents since they were eighteen. They had been jokers when we were younger, playing jokes on each other and me often.

This was probably just a joke. Their way of getting one more over me. It had to be a prank. If I brought it up, they'd likely laugh in my face and ask how I could possibly have thought they were serious.

Shaking my head, I hurried to shower and change for the party. It took me right up until Branson stomped up the stairs to get me to finish. Throwing my door open, I said, "I'm ready!"

He scowled at my glowing hair. "You okay?"

I nodded. "Just rushed."

He stepped to the side and let me out, scowling at the obvious lie, but not saying anything, thankfully.

CHAPTER
THREE

The royals threw the grandest parties ever and I loved every second of it. My grandparents and great grandparents took turns stealing me for hugs and discussions, all making me promise to visit soon now that I was back.

My dads took turns dancing with me and it wasn't long before my grandfathers did as well. I loved dancing with them, spinning around the room with the practiced classical dances they'd spent years teaching me as I grew up. Although I was a princess and taught all the etiquette expected of a princess, I was not expected to take over as queen. Something which I was extremely grateful for. However, I would do my part to help my clan and my brother when he ultimately became king.

My aunts, uncles, and their children bombarded me, but my brother rescued me, pulling me away and growling about how he was the last one to get to see me.

"Thank you," I breathed as I hugged him, safely out on a back patio in the cold night air.

"Don't thank me yet," he whispered and looked over my shoulder. "Just remember, I'm your only sibling and you'd be really sad if I was dead, so you can't kill me." He kissed my cheek and ran back inside to the party.

Scowling, I wondered what the heck that had been about. He wasn't normally so shifty or weird.

"Good evening, Princess," a deep, gravelly voice said behind me.

I froze in place, my heart, however, tripled in speed. No, it wasn't my birthday. Why was he here?

"Your hair looks good so long," he commented, his voice closer. "Don't you think so, Mas?"

"Hmph," Mason replied.

Closing my eyes, I willed the ability to teleport to suddenly present itself. Mom could do it, so maybe I could as well, even though we weren't blood related. Please? Please?

"Are you going to try to ignore us even in person?" Mason asked.

Summoning the resolve, I turned with a wide smile. "Mason! Kayden! Long time no see. How are you two? When did you get in town? I thought you lot were still on the other continent helping with the demon problem?"

They looked at each other, scowling, before turning to me.

"Did you not get our letter?" Kayden asked, walking closer.

Maya opened the patio door, looked around, and tensed when she saw the three of us. "Oh, uh, Lily, Great Nana Kara was asking for you. Should I tell her you're—"

"Coming!" I shouted and started towards the door,

turning my head, I smiled at Kayden and Mason. Stars they looked amazing. Tall, muscular, fierce, and handsome. Enough to make women everywhere drool, but right now I felt pain and fear. I needed to get away from them. "We'll have to catch up soon!" Once inside with the door separating them from me, I exhaled and said, "You are a lifesaver, Maya."

She shook her head as she led the way to the table where Great Nana Kara was sitting. "Those two are right behind us, girl. They aren't going to give up without you talking to them." We paused right near the table and she turned to me, her mouth dropped open. "Wait, is this about the promise?" she squeaked.

I put a hand over her mouth. "Shush. How did you even know about that?"

She pulled my hand down. "You told me when we were kids. I'd forgotten about it, but your twenty-fifth birthday is coming up next week." She gasped. "Is that why they're back? To mate with you?"

"Who's mating with whom?" Great Nana Kara asked.

Maya and I flinched.

"No one is mating with anybody, Nana," I said as I turned and smiled at her. She had a full head of grey hair now that was pulled back to show off her pointed ears. She always moved with elegance and was the epitome of royalty. She was also the best healer in the world. Hurrying over, I knelt by her chair to hug her. "How have you been?"

"I'm better now that you're back," she said. "I brought you here to discuss something important, though."

"Oh?" I asked and took the empty seat beside her.

"A little elven girl, full blooded elf, has shifted into a snake. Her parents asked if you might be willing to talk with her and help her."

"Of course!" I said, delighted. "Being a snake isn't the easiest, so we have to stick together."

She smiled and patted my cheek gently. "That's wonderful. Thank you. Are you having fun tonight?"

"Getting to spend time with my family is always fun," I said, and leaned into her hand.

She leaned closer and asked, "Is that why you ran away from Mason and Kayden?"

I opened my mouth to argue, but she winked at me and said, "Darling, can you go find your mother and let her know about the plans?"

"Of course, Great Nana," I said and stood. Out of the corner of my eye, I saw Mason and Kayden approaching.

"Kayden and Mason! Come give me a hug! How have two of my favorite boys been?" she yelled as I veered away from her and searched the room for my mom. My wonderful, wonderful great grandmother always had my back. I'd have to buy her a present and visit her soon.

I spotted Mom across the dance floor and started my way through the people, pushing through those dancing.

An arm looped around my waist and pulled me into a spinning dance.

Raising my eyes, I gasped when I found them connected with Prince Trey of the Dragons.

"Hello, Princess Liliana," he greeted with a warm smile.

"Prince Trey," I whispered in response and tried to break free from the dance, but he kept his hold on my waist.

"You've been ignoring our calls and messages for years. We've tried to figure out what we could have done to upset you so much, but keep coming up blank. So, can you enlighten me on what caused your sudden avoidance?" He was so calm and poised all the time. In moments like this, it pissed me off. How could he just ask that so bluntly, and as if he wasn't the one who had ignored me?

My hair glowed brighter and he noticed it, his grip loosening slightly.

Pulling out of his hold, I said, "If you'll excuse me, Your Highness, I have a message to deliver to my queen. Good night." Spinning on my heel, I marched the rest of the way to her, and everyone veered out of my path, all knowing what my glowing hair meant.

Mom was laughing at something Great Grandpa Dan had said, but her eyes looked at my hair and then at my face, and she was immediately on her feet. "Sweetheart, why don't we go outside and get some air?"

"I would like to go home," I said through clenched teeth. The darkness and anger swirled higher and higher, threatening to overtake me, causing my hair to glow even brighter. My tongue changed into my forked snake's tongue and I clenched my teeth to keep from hissing.

"What's going on?" Great Grandpa Dan asked. Ezio stood from his seat between him and Holly.

"Lily," Kayden called out.

"Mom!" I said urgently, hissing slightly.

Ezio looked at Kayden and then back at me, putting two and two together. He marched towards his son, snarling, and put a hand on his chest to stop him. "What's going on, Kay?"

Mom put her hand on my shoulder. "Please excuse us," Mom said with an apologetic smile, "the jet lag has gotten to us. Have a good evening."

Mason stepped forward with his mouth open, but Mom teleported us to the living room in the house.

"Lily, talk to me," she whispered softly and put her hands on my arms.

"I'm going to my rock," I said and headed upstairs to change out of my dress and into sweats and a tank top. Quickly, I went to the barn where a large rock designed to heat to whatever temperature I set it to was installed. My dads had installed it when I first moved in, but the rock and lamp had grown in size as I had.

Shifting into my snake form, I curled up on the warm rock and closed my eyes. Exhaling in relief, I realized that Great Uncle Silverowl was right, I had waited too long between shifts. It felt good to be in snake form.

Plus, the darkness was immediately back down, deep within my soul, slumbering as it should be, when I was in snake form.

Mom peeked her head in a bit later, but left me alone when she confirmed I was fine.

My brother Tony prowled inside in his wolf form, curled up at the foot of the rock, between the door and I, and went to sleep. Even though I was older by five years, he was very protective of me, and he likely felt bad for his part in the earlier incident.

With him nearby, my unease disappeared and I was finally able to sleep.

CHAPTER

FOUR

Everyone thankfully didn't bring up the incident at the party, though I could see they were curious.

Tony and I went to the square of our clan territory where several shops were open with delicious food and handcrafted items for sale.

My first stop was Kieran's store where he, his mate, and his mate's other mates baked delicious pastries.

Kieran lifted his eyes when he heard us come in and they widened when they saw me. "Lily! I didn't realize you were back already."

"Lily!" Kieran's mate, Sheila, yelled in excitement and raced towards me to hug me tightly. "You're back!"

I squeezed her and smiled with a nod. "I am."

She ran back behind the counter, grabbed a bag, and put a cinnamon roll, chocolate croissant, and two sweet purple yam rolls inside. "Here! Your favorites!"

Gasping in excitement, I grabbed the bag, pulled out a chocolate croissant, and bit into it. It was still warm! "So good!" I moaned. "You can't find pastries as good as this near my college. I tried a couple and it just made me cry and miss home and your bakery."

She put a hand to her chest and tears built in her eyes. "That means a lot to hear from you, Princess."

"Here," Kieran said and held out a bag for Tony. "I just baked some buttermilk biscuits, since I heard you were home."

"Thank you, Kieran!" Tony shouted and took the bag.

This was a very familiar scene, one that had happened at least a dozen times as we grew up. It felt nice to still experience it, even though I was an adult now. Hopefully, there were other things like this that wouldn't change as I got even older.

A familiar presence pressed upon me from the side, alerting me in advance of his approach. Sometimes it was good to be able to sense alphas and the signature auras of those you were familiar with. Though I wished I'd been able to sense them last night. Why hadn't I sensed them last night? Was it just because there had been so many alphas at the party?

"I hate to leave so quickly, but I've—"

"Oh, you don't have to explain to us!" Sheila said. "We know you're busy with all your duties. Thank you for coming to see us."

"I'll come by again soon," I promised as I backed out.

I closed the door just as Kayden and Mason entered the square. Tony turned me towards the house, in the opposite direction as Kayden, and pushed my lower back. "Go, I'll distract them. It's the least I can do after yesterday, but you and I are going to talk about why you're avoiding them later."

"Thank you," I whispered and walked confidently and calmly away, like I hadn't noticed them coming.

"Lily!" Kayden called out.

"Kay!" Tony yelled. "Where have you been, man? We have got to catch up. Where's Trey?"

"Not now, Tony. We need to talk to—"

"Kayden!" Kieran yelled. "Come inside! We've got a bag for you. Wow, it's been so long since we saw you. How have you been?"

Thank you, Kieran for the assist!

Branson, stepped out from behind one of the buildings, following me. "Let's talk, Daughter."

"Um, could we not?" I asked and cringed.

"If you want help avoiding them, then you've got to talk to me," he said. "Also, you're twenty-four, almost twenty-five years old. Why are you acting like a teenager?"

Ouch, that was Bran Bran, straight to the heart of the problem.

"I don't want to discuss it," I said. "I just need a bit more time away from them to collect my thoughts. Okay?"

He sighed. "Fine, whenever you're ready, I'll listen, okay? Now, do you want me to chase them away?"

"Tony said he was—"

"Lily!" Mason snarled.

I yelped.

Bran Bran growled softly. "Go to the house. Your mother has some questions about your party that you need to answer."

"Love you," I whispered and ran towards the house.

"Branson," Mason growled. "We just need—"

"You need to rethink your approach to me, pup," Branson growled.

The door safely shut behind me, I raised my eyes to meet Mom's wide ones. "Uh, Bran Bran said you needed to ask me some questions?"

She stood at the island, eating a breakfast sandwich. Flipping around a tablet, she tapped it. "I need you to answer these questions so I can finalize your party details."

"About that, do we really need a party? Maybe we could just go out to dinner as a family or—"

"Lily, what is going on? You've been acting strange ever since the party yesterday." She folded her arms and said, "Your hair has been glowing almost nonstop."

"Something stressful is happening, but I'm going to deal with it soon, I promise. The hair is just reacting to my stress, that's all. No anger. Promise." Taking a deep breath, I reminded myself that this wasn't a problem and would be fixed soon. I drew in the scent of my house, my mom, and let the anxiety drain away. When my eyes opened, I could see the strands, no longer glowing. "See?"

Mom continued to scowl, but just tapped the tablet. "Answers, please."

Giving in, I looked over the questions, mostly about colors and theme, and answered them so the party planner could set things up for the party. Normally, we wouldn't have had such a big one, but it was a dual birthday and graduation party, so they were going all out.

"Do we need to edit the guest list?" she asked with an arched brow.

I flinched. "No, it's fine." As much as I wanted to avoid talking to them, I knew I needed to. I knew we would have to hash out our issues soon. I couldn't keep running from them. I was an adult, after all. But even though it had been years, I hadn't prepared myself for how to respond to them when my heart still hurt.

"Okay. Now, how about you bring that bag of delicious pastries this way and share with your mom?" she wiggled her fingers at my bag.

Clutching it against my chest, I backed up. "No, these are mine! Go get your own."

"Oh, come on. Don't be stingy. Just one?" She walked around the island, hands out.

"No!" I snapped and ran out of the kitchen, but she wrapped her arms around me just before the living room, making me squeal.

"Share!" she yelled. "Why are you and your brother so stingy and never share? I thought I raised you better than that?"

Tony opened the door, saw us struggling for the bag, and slowly backed out.

"He has a bag, too!" I yelled.

Mom gasped, released me, and ran out the front door. "Tony! Come back!"

Shaking my head while laughing, I made my way up to my room, sat on my bed, and ate my pastries. I spent the remainder of my day hiding in my room, catching up on emails and watching the local news to find out the most talked about things. Often, the human newscasters discussed things that the other races didn't, so I felt it was good to know as much as I could.

The demon problem was spreading and the humans were starting to get scared. Was there a way to stop them?

My phone beeped and I opened it to a message from Maya.

MAYA: *Club. Tonight?*
    Me: *Yes!*
    Maya: *Pick me up at 8.*
    Me: *It's a date!*

JUMPING TO MY FEET, I rushed to my closet to pick out a dress for the club. My club appropriate attire was severely lacking though. Heading to Mom's room, I knocked, but she didn't answer.

"Mom?" I called loud enough she should have heard me from anywhere in the house.

No answer.

Shrugging, I opened the door to her room, peeked to make sure no one was inside, then hurried to her closet to borrow a dress.

She had tons of dresses, many gifted to her by Great Aunt Leona and Nana Jolie. A bright green dress in the back caught my eye. It was long-sleeved, had a lowcut front, and was styled to look scrunched on the sides. It was thigh length and absolutely perfect for the club. Grabbing it, I spun around, and screamed when I came face to face with Dad.

His lips twitched as he fought a smile. "Going out?"

"You scared ten years off of my life," I gasped, bent over, and panted. "Why did you sneak up on me like that?"

"I didn't sneak up on you, you should have heard me, but clearly were too absorbed with picking out a dress." Leaning a shoulder against the wall, he asked, "Are you ever going to talk about what's going on with you and your former best friends?"

"No," I said as I straightened. "Thanks for asking, though."

He sighed and shook his head. "I don't know what those boys did, but try to remember that being an alpha, especially one who is out fighting to protect others, makes your emotions run high at times and can cause you to say things in a heated moment you don't mean."

Looking up at him, I asked, "If Mom had ignored your calls and messages for more than a few days, more than a few months or even years, what would you have done?"

"Gone to find her and demanded to know why she was ignoring me," he said without hesitation. "Apologized for what I had done wrong or tried to find a way to fix it."

I nodded. "That's what I thought. And that is *not* what they did."

He frowned and said, "There are times when duty makes doing things like that difficult."

Sighing, I set my hand on his shoulder as I stepped up next to him and said, "Don't try to give them an out, Dad. They are adults, grown males, who will have to live with their consequences. They had plenty of time to reach out, to try to mend the break in our friendship. To find me at the college they knew the location of and talk to me. It's not your job to try to convince me to give them a second chance, not that they want or deserve one."

"Everyone deserves a second chance, cub. If your mother hadn't given me a second chance, we might not be mates right now."

Rolling my eyes, I shook my head. "Everyone knew you were meant to be together. The trio and I aren't soulmates or matches like you guys are."

"Whatever is going on between you four, just do me a favor and give them one chance to explain themselves. If they shoot themselves in the foot with their explanation, or it's a terrible one, then write them off and move on. I'm not saying I think you guys should be together, but I know when I was a prince, an alpha who spent a lot of years doing what was needed, that sometimes doing what you want isn't easy. Okay?"

I gave him a kiss on the cheek and said, "Okay, Dad."

"Do you need a driver?" he asked as I headed out of the room.

"Yes. I need to pick up Maya before we go out."

He pulled out his phone and nodded. "On it."

"You're the best!" I called over my shoulder as I hurried to my room to get ready.

Maybe Dad was right. Maybe I should give them a chance to explain everything. However, tonight was a night for fun and the serious discussions could wait until tomorrow … or next week.

Running down the stairs, I yelled bye to everyone, ignoring their calls to come back so they couldn't try to parent me when I was a grown adult. Outside, Ezio stood next to a black SUV wearing black slacks and a shiny black button-up shirt.

"You clean up nice, old man," I teased.

He lifted his lip in a snarl. "Watch it, pup, or I'll let you walk."

Climbing into the passenger seat, I messaged Maya to let her know we were on our way.

"Which club are you going to?" he asked as he started the vehicle.

"That new one that just opened, Dynamite? Or Dynamic?" It was something like that.

"Dynamo," Ezio answered. "Did you know that's owned by your Great Uncle Gavin?"

Shit, if it was owned by Gavin, did that mean Trey would be there?

"I did *not* know that," I admitted softly.

"When we get to Maya's, I'll message the bouncer to get you two on the list. He's from our clan, so I can message him and ensure we don't have any issues when we show up," he said.

"Thanks, Ezio," I said with a smile. "It's been a few years since I've been out to a club. I heard this one was really nice and Maya and I have been talking about visiting for months."

"It is a really nice place. The music is loud, but not so loud it hurts our sensitive ears. And, they have some really delicious drinks."

I looked up from my phone to stare at him. "You've been?"

He smiled. "I may be old, but I'm not dead, Lily. Holly and I have gone a few times. Gavin actually invited the entire hybrid clan to opening night."

He had? Maya never told me about that.

We pulled up to Maya's house, but she was already outside, wearing a killer purple miniskirt and a top that tied around her chest, exposing her stomach and her cleavage.

"You look great!" I chirped as she climbed in and hugged me.

"You, too! That color looks amazing on you."

"Ezio is getting us added to the list," I explained when she glanced at Ezio with his head down, texting on his phone. "Why didn't you tell me that our clan got to go for opening night?"

"I didn't want you to feel bad or try to convince me to go since I'd already promised to go with you," she said and smiled. "The wait will be worth it, I'm sure."

"Okay, you two are on the list and he's been advised that I'm coming as well. He said they've got an open VIP booth, if you want it?"

"Yes!" Maya and I shouted simultaneously.

Ezio smiled. "I thought so." He typed again on his phone, waited until it pinged, nodded, and put it down to drive again. "Okay, VIP table has been secured. Let's go!"

"Are you going to sit with us or act all bodyguard like?" Maya asked.

"My job tonight is to keep you two safe," he said with a scowl. "Sitting in the booth with you, drinking and having fun, prevents me from surveilling the surroundings to keep you out of danger."

"One of these days, we're going to convince you to enjoy the night with us," Maya said. "Maybe after Lily finds a mate who can take over guard duty."

Ezio growled. "She's got plenty of time before she needs to settle down."

Maya scoffed. "You're even worse than her dad!"

"What about you, hm? How's the mate hunt going on your end?" Ezio asked, diverting the topic from me.

"Aren't guards supposed to be silent?" she muttered, earning a hearty laugh from him.

CHAPTER
FIVE

The club had a line that wrapped around the block, so I was thankful for my celebrity status as Princess of the Hybrids allowing me to be driven right up to the door and let in.

Cameras flashed and people called out to me, some trying to get me to sign things.

I waved and smiled to everyone, but continued my walk up to the door with Maya at my side.

Ezio bumped fists with the bouncer, who dipped his head to me as we walked in.

Another bouncer met us inside and led us to the VIP section, where we got a large table with a plush couch around it roped off from the rest of the club. All eyes turned to us as we walked in and sat down.

Maya preened under the attention, looking for her first dance partner. "Maybe I should start with a non-alpha to switch things up a bit?"

I rolled my eyes, but before I could respond, our waiter approached.

He was a handsome elf with slightly pointed ears, blonde hair so light it was almost white, and a sharp jawline and cheekbones. "Good evening, Your Highness," he greeted me with a deep bow. "I am Tony and I'll be taking care of you tonight."

Immediately, my excitement over him was doused with his name being the same as my brother's. Giving him a kind smile, I said, "It's nice to meet you, Tony. Can you bring us a bottle of your best sparkling wine and a cup of cherries?"

He bowed. "I shall return quickly, but please do not wait for me. You are free to explore the club and I will bring your drinks and ensure no one enters your booth."

"We are here with Ezio of the Werewolves," I said quickly. "He is our guard for the night."

He nodded. "I know Ezio, so I will be sure to allow him entrance."

He turned to Maya. "Is there anything else you would like, Maya?"

She flushed and said, "Some waters would be great, too."

He bowed with a grand flourish. "I shall bring you both waters with lemon, light ice, as you prefer."

After he left the area, I grabbed her arm and said, "You've been holding out on me, wench! How does he know what your preferred water is?"

"I met him while you were gone," she whispered. "We went on two dates and then I got busy with work."

"And why are you not dating that handsome elf now?" I asked, mouth open in disbelief. He was one hundred percent her type!

"I get nervous when I'm with him because he's so hot!" she shouted and puffed her cheeks out. "There, are you happy?"

"You're going to ask him out on a date before we leave tonight," I said without room for rebuttal.

She smirked. "Well, twist my arm, why don't you?"

Ezio circled the room, getting a feel for everyone in the club and for anyone who might be trouble. He had a keen sense for malice, something that came in really useful when he'd been my guard.

We had to wait until he finished his route before we could go to the dance floor. I didn't mind waiting. Honestly, a drink first would be nice anyway.

Looking around the club, I was relieved to not see anyone that I knew. Even though everyone knew who I was, most would be too intimidated to come talk to me, so tonight would hopefully be a relatively uneventful and fun night.

Tony returned with our bottle of sparkling wine, two flute glasses, a cup of cherries, and two water glasses with lemon and just a little bit of ice. "Here are your drinks and the cherries as requested. Is there anything else I can get you lovely ladies?"

"How about a date for tomorrow?" I asked with a smile. "My friend here happens to be free about six o'clock."

Her face turned as red as her hair.

He looked at Maya and said, "I work until six, but could pick you up at seven for dinner."

Her eyes widened and she nodded. "Okay."

Smiling, he said, "Great. I'll text you after my shift

tonight so we can finalize the details." He turned, winked at me, and mouthed, "thank you," before he walked to the back of our area in the shadowy part to wait for us to need him again.

Maya put two cherries in each of the flute glasses, poured the sparkling wine in, and handed me one of the glasses. "Drink up, bitch!"

I clinked my glass against hers, took a drink, and moaned. "So tasty."

We watched the people dancing while we finished our drink and I poured us a second one. This time, I looked at the other VIP areas. My eyes widened at the sight of some of my second cousins in somewhat compromising positions. I would never act that way in a public setting where anyone could take pictures. They should know better!

"Okay, this is the plan," Maya said as she looked out over the dancers, snagging my attention. "You and I are going to go dance in the center and let those who are confident enough come try to dance with us."

"I like this plan," I agreed with a nod.

Ezio gave us a thumbs up before moving to the shadows next to Tony.

"Alright! Let's get this party started!" I said, downed the rest of my drink, ate my cherries, and headed towards the rope and the bouncer stationed there.

The bouncer, a werewolf Great Grandpa Dan took on a lot of missions, bowed his head to me. "Princess," he greeted.

"We're going to go dance," I informed him. "Ezio is here."

He nodded. "I sensed and saw him." Unhooking the rope,

he pulled it back so we could step down. "Just call out if you need anything."

"Thanks," I chirped as I skipped by him with Maya right on my heels.

"Maybe I should look for a werewolf. They seem to be the more polite of all the races towards women," she whispered.

Focusing on the powers of those around me, I searched for the most powerful beings in the room. There were several really strong alphas along the edges of the room, the guards like Ezio, but interspersed throughout the dancefloor were a handful as well. In the middle, I spotted a handsome, tall man with dark, wavy hair dancing while talking to a man next to him, who was not as powerful, but definitely still an alpha.

Bingo. "Follow me," I ordered Maya and started dancing my way through the crowd to get closer to them. When I was a few people away, I grabbed Maya and we danced together, waiting for them to take notice of us.

It didn't take long and, unsurprisingly, the slightly weaker alpha came over to dance with Maya first. In my experience, they liked to send in their wingman first before making their move.

The tall, dark-haired alpha approached me. He danced around me, smiling, and clearly having a good time. My smile mirrored his as we danced together, the song fast and fun.

"I didn't expect to have a dance with royalty tonight," he said in my ear as we danced.

"I guess it's just your lucky day," I teased and spun in a circle.

His warm hands rested on my stomach as he moved closer behind me. "You're even more beautiful in person than on TV," he said, his warm breath blowing across the shell of my ear and making me shiver.

"I'm at a disadvantage," I said. "You know my name, but I don't know yours."

"Unimportant," a deep, rumbling voice said as the man I'd been dancing with was pulled away from me suddenly.

Heart hammering, I spun around to see Mason glaring at the guy I had been dancing with.

"Who are you?" the guy asked and looked at me. "I know she's unmated."

"Beat it," Mason growled. "You're not worthy of breathing the same air as her."

My eyes widened. Was that a compliment? Was Mason saying something nice about me in public where others could hear him?

Maya slowly backed her and her dance partner away to avoid the fall out.

"What are you doing, Mason?"

"Me? What are you doing?" he snapped.

"Until you showed up, I was enjoying myself," I snapped back. My hair started to glow as the rage awakened within me.

Mason's eyes darted to my hair before he scowled and said, "You're ignoring us, but you're dancing with a loser like this?"

"What'd you call me?" the guy asked and took a step closer to Mason, his chest puffed up.

I raised one of my hands straight up into the air.

Within seconds, Ezio was there. "Let's take a breath," Ezio said to the guy. "Let me tell you that fighting is not the way to the princess's heart, and you really do not want to fight Mason."

Situation under control thanks to Ezio, I turned and headed towards our booth. I groaned when I saw Trey and Kayden in the booth, sipping on my sparkling wine.

I glanced at the werewolf bouncer, who shrugged and said, "You try to keep them out of somewhere."

Patting his arm as I walked by, I said, "No worries, I know they're stubborn jerks on the best of days."

He snickered, but quickly stopped and resumed looking stoic as he clipped the rope behind me.

Stomping up to the booth, I folded my arms across my chest and asked, "What do you want? I was enjoying my night out until you lot showed up."

"This is my father's club," Trey reminded me. "Did you think word wouldn't reach me that you were here?"

Sitting down, I picked up the bottle and drank straight from it. "Why do you care if I'm here or not? We haven't spoken in years."

"And whose fault is that?" Kayden asked and glared at me.

My hair was glowing so brightly that our dark area was bright as noon instead. "Fine, you don't want me dancing here, I'll go somewhere else," I said and stood.

"You can keep avoiding us, but eventually, we're going to talk," Trey said calmly, his leg crossed over the other as he leaned back, looking regal and confident. "We know where you live and we have plenty of people around the city who will update us on your location."

"Why do you care?" I shouted. "Why are you interrupting me trying to enjoy myself? Why do you care if I dance with a random alpha or date or anything? You haven't cared the last four years!"

"Because you made a promise," Kayden said. "And I know you haven't forgotten, even if you are pretending you didn't read our letter."

I shook my head. "I read your letter and knew you were all just going to laugh at me if I brought it up, knowing you weren't serious. Knowing that you were just doing something to ruffle my scales like you always used to."

Trey sat up, his face completely serious as he said, "On the contrary, Princess, we are very serious about following up on our promise. On making you our mate."

My eyes widened at the sincerity in his voice. Were they serious? No, they couldn't be. And yet, I hadn't sensed a lie when he had spoken just now.

Laughing, I shook my head. "You almost got me, Trey. You've always had the best poker face." Taking another drink of the bottle of sparkling wine, I set it down, stood, and turned away from them. "Have a good evening."

Kayden grabbed my wrist, stopping me. "Lily, what did we do? Why have you been ignoring us all these years?"

"You really want to know?" I asked softly. The fury within me grew, my hair glowing the brightest it ever had. Fury at their games. Fury at the pain I'd felt from the message that caused the rift between us. Fury at still caring about them.

"Yes, that's why we asked," Trey said calmly.

"Because I realized that I had been completely wrong about how you felt about me. That you didn't care about me like you claimed!" I shouted.

Kayden's eyes widened at my hostility.

I jerked my wrist free of his grasp and continued, "I thought we were best friends. I thought you cared, but you told me, 'I never considered you my sister!'"

Ezio and Maya had returned and at my statement, Ezio moved closer, eyes wide.

Kayden's brows rose. "*That's* what caused you to stop talking to us? Because I admitted I never considered you my sister?" He stared at me a second, then threw his head back and laughed.

The asshole actually laughed at me.

Trey and Mason also joined in on the laughter. Trey shook his head as he laughed at me.

"Fuck you, Kayden. Fuck all of you!" My anger was so strong that it was palpable and electricity began to zap around me. Spinning on my heel, I headed towards the exit. "I'm going home."

"Lily," Kayden said around his laughs, "wait."

"Enough," Ezio growled. "What is wrong with you? Why are you treating her like this?"

"You don't understand," Kayden began, but I made my way out of the club so I didn't have to hear anymore.

Maya walked at my side, glancing at me nervously. "I love you, Lil."

"I need to kill something," I hissed, my tongue shifting into my snake's forked form.

"Okay," she said with a nod. "Let's go hunting."

With Ezio dealing with Kayden, we didn't have a driver, so we needed a cab. The bouncer at the entrance looked behind me and frowned when he didn't see Ezio.

"Cab, please," I said through clenched teeth.

He nodded, raised his arm, and bowed to me as the cab pulled up. "Thank you for visiting our establishment, Princess. I hope to see you again."

"Thank you," I said, trying to be as civil as I could when nothing but fury flowed through me. My skin itched, wanting to shift.

He opened the backdoor of the cab and closed it after Maya and I were inside, continuing to bow.

Maya gave the driver the address, since it was becoming more and more difficult to speak. My body ached as I held back from shifting. I knew the driver wouldn't be too happy with a twenty-foot snake in his car, which meant shifting was out of the question.

"Almost there," Maya whispered and smiled. "Almost, Lil."

How could he laugh at me? I finally admitted what they said that had hurt my feelings and they had laughed.

Scales rippled along my skin and my jaw ached as it tried to shift.

Maya ordered the cab to stop in the middle of the road a mile from the house, but along the edge of our clan's property. She opened the door and waved me out.

The driver sped away as soon as I was out of the car. Running through the wards, I headed into the woods, searching for an animal to hunt.

Maya shifted into her bird form, but kept her fire minimal, and flew overhead, using her eyesight to help my search.

Movement to my left.

Shifting into my full snake form, I moved silently along the ground until I found just what I needed. A badger ripe for eating. With a quick strike, I bit down on it and coiled around him as tightly as I could.

CHAPTER
SIX

Mom and my dads took turns coming to check on me where I lay curled up on the forest floor, digesting the badger, over the next couple of days. Maya had let them know where I was, but I had no idea if she'd told them what had happened.

Honestly, it didn't matter since Ezio knew now.

As the morning sun rose on the third day, the day before my birthday, I shifted and walked towards the house, taking a deep breath as I prepared for the barrage of questions.

Pushing open the door, I quickly realized that no one was home. I hurried to my room and grabbed my cell phone to check for messages. There was just one from Mom telling me they were going to the werewolf Den, the werewolves' territory where they had their own city for the werewolves who didn't want to or weren't yet ready to be around the other races. My parents had left only an hour ago, which meant I could take a shower and change before meeting up with them there.

The hot shower felt good on my cold skin and I stood for several long minutes under the hot water. The anger I'd felt was gone, but the pain in my chest hadn't lessened.

After the shower, I meditated for an hour before dressing and heading to the garage to drive Mom's car.

I called Mom as I drove towards the gate.

"Hey!" she answered happily. "How's it going?"

"I'm on the way to the Den," I replied as happily as she had answered.

"Great! Dan will be excited to see you."

"Okay, love you, bye."

"Love you, too."

I called Maya next and as soon as she answered I apologized.

"Girl, you do not need to apologize. I'm still mad at them." She huffed.

Smiling, I could picture her annoyed face right now. "I love you."

"Love you, too. So, what are your plans for today?"

"Going to meet my parents at the Den. Want to come?"

"Yes! I'll be ready in five!" She hung up on me without waiting for my answer, which just made me laugh and shake my head.

Altering my course, I stopped at her house first to pick her up, then we drove to the Den. As soon as I parked in front of the main house, Great Grandpa Dan walked out and opened his arms.

Maya and I ran forward and hugged each side of the large werewolf who was the former king, and one of the sweetest males I knew.

"There are my girls!" he boomed and squeezed us. "I was debating ordering Ezio to kidnap you just so I could visit with you."

I patted his back before stepping back to look up at the large man with a full head of grey hair. "Sorry, Great Grandpa. Things have been ... busy."

He patted the top of my head, just like he'd been doing since I was five years old, and smiled. "Who do I need to bite?"

"Kayden and his pack," Maya grumbled.

Turning my head to the side, I glared at her and she put her hands over her mouth.

"Kayden? What has that headstrong pup done now?"

"Nothing, Great Grandpa. Don't worry about it," I said, and sighed as I shook my head. "It's best if we just forget about them for now."

His eyes narrowed. "That may be a bit hard to do, pup."

I turned to see what he was looking at and groaned. Kayden, Trey, and Mason all climbed out of an SUV with Ezio as the driver, their car parked behind mine.

"Freaking great," I muttered. Turning back around, I asked, "Where's Mom?"

"The barns," he answered.

Sighing, I rubbed my face with my hands. I couldn't go to the barns because the animals were all scared of me.

"My dads?"

"The market," he answered and stepped past me to intercept Kayden. "You and I can hang out later. Go on."

Hopping up, I kissed his cheek and whispered a quick thanks before grabbing Maya's hand and jogging towards the main part of the Den where the open-air market with vendors was.

Bran Bran stood in line at the meat stick seller and raised his arm when he saw me. "Hey, kiddo."

"Hey, Bran Bran," I greeted as I jogged over with a smile to hug him. Maya hugged him next and we joined him in line. "I'm starving."

"Well, you came at the right time," he said with a chuckle. "I was sent here to get food for your mom. So, I can get you some food, too."

"I'll go get bread so you don't have to wait in two lines," I said and headed to the next vendor who sold delicious, fluffy breads.

"I'm going to get drinks," Maya announced and jogged over to the last food vendor who made smoothies, boba drinks, and also sold waters and teas.

Once we had purchased everything, we followed Bran Bran to a grassy area where several others were sitting on the grass eating or just hanging out. Mom and my other dads were sitting on a large blanket that we joined them on.

"Hello, girls," Triston greeted Maya and I.

"You look refreshed," Riddick said.

"I had a good meditation session," I said with a smile, hoping they would drop the conversation, but as with many things in my life, it wasn't that easy.

"Hello," Trey said as he sat down beside me on my right side, crossing his legs.

Mason sat on Trey's right.

Kayden sat down on Maya's left, earning a glare from her.

"How are you boys?" Mom asked. She glanced at me, but kept an easy smile as she focused on them.

Grabbing one of the meat sticks, I tore a piece off while looking at the blanket just in front of me. I should have known Great Grandpa Dan wouldn't be able to keep them busy forever. Why were they even here? Why were they bothering me?

"Things have been busy," Trey said.

"How's your dad doing?" Caleb asked.

Pulling out my phone, I looked up the most recent news stories to distract myself from their conversations. There wasn't much going on, which was good.

Maya leaned her shoulder against mine, giving me silent comfort.

A strange, dark feeling hit me, making me jerk my eyes up.

Mom turned around as well, getting to her feet slowly. "Something's coming," she said and tapped Caleb on the shoulder.

I was on my feet, moving forward, but Mason stepped in front of me and put an arm out to stop me.

"What?" I asked, looking up at his scowling face.

His eyes darted to my face before looking back away from me. "I can smell demons."

Kayden stepped up next to me and said, "Get back. We'll handle this." He shifted into a warrior form of half wolf and half man.

Arguing would have felt good, but this was their job, so I went back to the blanket and sat beside Maya. "Guess we'll get to see if they're as good as they claim they are," I whispered to her.

Trey looked over his shoulder at me and winked, "Enjoy the show, Princess."

I rolled my eyes and grabbed my boba drink.

A black oval made of swirling smoke appeared in front of Mason and Kayden and several demonic creatures jumped out. They were only about three feet tall, covered in scales, and scurried around on all fours. When they howled at us, they revealed thick fangs on the top and bottom of their jaws.

Mason drew a sword from a scabbard on his back that I hadn't noticed and immediately decapitated one of the creatures. A thrill went through me that I didn't want to admit.

My dads and Mom created a shield between the guys and us, so I sat calmly with Maya to watch, knowing they would keep us safe.

"Have you ever wondered what would happen if you jumped through the portal?" Maya asked.

I nodded. "I assume you'd get teleported to their world."

"Do you think it's just a vast landscape of creatures that are attacking each other and these are weird anomalies sending them here?"

"Or, are there sentient beings sending the creatures here as a test to see if we're worth their time and energy or if they could colonize us?" I suggested.

"Oh, that's a scary thought," she said and shuddered.

Kayden and Mason attacked two creatures while Trey watched. Was he just going to make them do all the work?

Three more creatures jumped out and finally, Trey intervened, taking a warrior form to let his dragon side out, and spewed flames that coated one of the demonic creatures that looked like a dog with porcupine spines and we called a hell-hound. It was apparently a term used in some mythology.

My body warmed as I watched the trio protecting us from the demonic creatures. I knew they were skilled fighters, but knowing and watching them in action were two different things. The darkness within me swirled higher, trying to over-take me and summoning some of my bloodlust.

No! No, I could not get out of control. I had to stop it before anyone noticed.

Closing my eyes, I took deep breaths and thought of the pond and rock in the barn, my safe place, and thankfully, the darkness receded, taking my bloodlust with it.

I opened my eyes as the black portal disappeared. When they killed the last creature, all of the bodies went up in a black poof of smoke.

Why did some demon bodies disappear while other times they had to be burned to destroy the body? There were so many questions and we had so few answers.

Standing, I dusted myself off, tapped Maya to get her to follow, and headed to browse the vendors' stands. "Well, that was a bit anticlimactic," I said despite actually being impressed with how efficiently they had handled the crea tures and how I had reacted to them.

Maya gasped as she ran up to the first vendor selling hand carved jewelry boxes. "I've been wanting one of these!" She squatted down so she could look at them closer. "Which is your favorite?" she asked me.

I squatted next to her and pointed at the jewelry box with stars and hearts carved in it. "This one is my favorite."

"This one is mine," she said and pointed at one with a moon and two wolves howling at it.

The seller, an older man with grey at his temples, smiled. "I'm glad you like my work, Princess."

"You're very talented," I said and returned the smile. "How much are they?"

"Fifty," he answered.

"Oh, shoot. I only have forty on me," Maya said and pouted.

"Here," Trey said, and set a one hundred dollar bill on the table. "Consider it an apology gift for you both for disrupting your dancing last night."

The vendor took the cash, picked up the boxes, quickly wrapped them, and put them in a bag. "Thank you for your patronage, Prince Trey."

Telling him to take his gift and shove it would upset the vendor who was just trying to make a living, but I also didn't want to let him off so easy. So, I just turned and headed to the next vendor without responding or grabbing the bag, forcing Trey to carry it.

"You can't ignore us forever," Kayden said from beside me as I looked at earrings and a necklace that would go really well with my birthday dress.

"How much are these?" I asked the teenage girl who was manning the booth.

Her eyes were focused on Kayden, which I totally understood. He was handsome and powerful. Even reining in his power, he oozed a bit that made you take notice of him.

"Miss?" I asked, finally getting her attention.

She flushed and said, "Forty for the set."

I pulled out the cash from my pocket, but before I could pay her, Kayden gave her a fifty, winked, and said, "Keep the change."

Growling, I turned and glared up at him. "Buying me gifts isn't going to make me forgive you or want to talk to you. So, stop."

"But it did get you to talk to me, finally," he said. "And you stopped running away."

"Would you want to be around someone who laughed at you when you tried to be open about your feelings?"

"About that." He rubbed the back of his neck, his cheeks turning slightly pink. "You misunderstood what I was saying and why I laughed. I wasn't laughing at you, Lily."

Scoffing, I spun away from him, grabbed the bag the girl had ready with the jewelry, and moved to the next vendor. "Leave me alone. I don't want to talk to you or your pack."

"Why are you so damn stubborn?" he growled.

"Leave her alone, Kayden," Maya snapped and stepped behind me to block him. "You're an asshole and she doesn't want to talk to you."

"I'm not an asshole. She misunderstood and if you'd just let me—"

"This is not the right location for this type of conversation," Mom said sternly from behind us. "Lily, go hear them out."

"No," I hissed as I turned to face her. "I won't hear them out. In fact, I'm done seeing them. You're not welcome around me, so piss off." Grabbing the bags from Trey's hands,

I walked away, but didn't get far before Ezio of all people stopped me.

"This is one of those times when you really just need to listen," he said softly. "I grilled them last night and you just need to hear them out."

"Even you?" I asked and shook my head. "Well, he is your son, so I suppose that makes sense."

"Lily, you're being childish," Ezio said. "Why won't you let them explain?"

"Because they had four years to explain. Because they laughed at my pain." The anger started to build, but I closed my eyes, took a cleansing breath, and said, "Fine, I'll hear them out."

Ezio smiled, but my next sentence ended that.

"In four years, they can come find me and explain then."

Was I being childish? Yes. Was I going to stop? I couldn't. Even if my hair wasn't glowing, I was too angry and hurt to face them right now.

Maya looped her arm through mine and we headed out to the car. I dropped her off at her place and went back home, locking myself in my room to take a nap.

I was almost asleep when Kayden jumped through my window.

Screaming, I threw a pillow at him before I realized who it was.

"What are you doing?" I demanded.

He caught the pillow and smiled at the snake embroidered on it, a gift he'd given me when we were kids. "I used to sneak in through the window when we were younger all the time."

"When we were *kids*. Why are you doing it now?"

"You locked the doors," he replied, and looked over at the envelope on my desk. Smirking he said, "So, you did read it."

"I told you I don't want to talk," I snapped and sat on my bed with my legs crossed in front of me.

He sat on the edge of my bed and looked at the pillow still in his hands. "My dad always loved you. I used to think he loved you more than me, but as I grew older, I realized he loved you in a different way than he loved me."

We'd gotten into fights a few times over that topic.

Looking up at me he said, "As I got older, I realized that how I felt about you was different, too. I don't view you as a sister, Lily, because I view you as a packmate, as a potential mate. Because I am interested in you. That's definitely not how siblings feel for each other."

Blinking in disbelief I asked, "Interested in me?"

He walked over to the desk, picked up the envelope, and said, "We're serious, Lily. About this promise. About wanting you as a mate."

Had I heard him correctly? Really? That was what the idiot had meant by that text?

"Don't joke with me," I said softly as I stood and backed towards the door. "It's not funny to play games like that."

"I'm not playing games," he said and waved the envelope at me. "We're serious."

"You're serious about a promise we made when you were six years old?" I arched a brow and crossed my arms over my chest.

"Why are you still single, Lily? You're a beautiful, smart

princess. Surely there were guys vying for your attention while you were at college, right?"

"What I did or didn't do is none of your business." Why was it hard to swallow right now? Why was my heart beating so fast?

He stalked closer to me and I backed up until I hit the door and he caged me in. "I know you're attracted to us. I know you want me just like I want you. Mason may be blind, but I'm not. I see the way you look at us, how you've looked at us since at least high school. You didn't get hurt because you wanted me to think of you as my sister. You got your feelings hurt because you thought I meant I didn't care about you at all. Do you know what thought gets me through every demon battle?"

Against my attempt not to, I asked, "What?"

"Knowing that you're out here, waiting for me, for us. That killing those demons helps keep *you* safe."

I shook my head. "I haven't been waiting for—"

He pressed his lips against mine and I froze, shocked by the move. The darkness within me swirled in my core and a similar darkness swirled in Kayden's aura. He pulled back slowly and said, "I'm sorry I hurt your feelings. That wasn't my intention. I laughed because it was such a simple misunderstanding. Because it was so absurd that you would think I had meant I don't care about you when it was the opposite. But of course, you're so stubborn, so we've been spending all this time chasing you."

"You could have come to see me. You knew where my college was." Sure, they were busy fighting demons around the world and doing Trey's princely duties, but they could have made time to come by for a single day.

He shook his head. "I was too scared."

"Scared of what?" He was one of the most fearless people I knew.

"Of seeing you with some guy."

Laughter burst out of me before I could stop it.

He scowled. "Now who is laughing at who?"

"You could have called me."

"You blocked our numbers."

Oh, right. I had.

"So, tell me, Princess, are you going to follow through on your promise?"

Follow through on taking them as mates? Without even courting? Yes, I was attracted to them, but we'd been apart four years. People changed a lot over four years.

"You want to follow through on our promise to be mates?" I asked. "How do I know you three aren't just doing this to laugh at me if I did say I would follow through on it?"

He opened his mouth, but my phone rang, interrupting him.

I pulled it out and frowned at the name. Luca, a dragon from college who had tried to date me, but I had continually turned down. "Hello?" I answered.

"Lily!" he replied loudly, making me pull the phone away from my ear. "How's the most beautiful woman in the world doing?"

Kayden's eyes darkened as he glared at my phone.

"What's up, Luca?" Turning my back on Kayden, I

walked over to my closet to get some space from him. The distraction was nice, giving me time to breathe and think about what Kayden had said and how my darkness reacted to him.

"I just wanted to let you know that I will be at your party tomorrow and I've got an awesome gift for you. So, prepare to be impressed."

"Oh, uh, you didn't have to get me anything, Luca. And I thought you'd said you were going to be with your family so you couldn't attend the party?"

"What kind of man would I be if I didn't come to your party? I let my family know I would be gone for a few days and when I explained why, they were totally fine with it."

"Oh, well, great. I'll see you tomorrow then."

"Have a great day, beautiful!"

I hung up the phone and turned around, but Kayden was gone.

"What the heck? Kay?" Sticking my head out my window, I saw him running in the direction of his dad's house. "Huh? Maybe his dad or mom needed him." I shrugged and decided it wasn't my problem.

My problem was realizing that it seemed like they were serious about the promise and needing to figure out what I was going to do about it. I also needed to get the feeling of Kayden's lips on mine out of my head.

"Lily!" Mom yelled from downstairs making me yelp and jump in surprise because I hadn't heard them come home. "Time to go pick up your dress."

I grabbed the jewelry and my shoes from my closet and called back, "Coming!"

As we drove to the store, Mom asked, "Do I need to cross them off the guest list?"

"No," I said and shook my head.

"Good," she said with a nod. "Next time, tell Kayden to use the front door. He always leaves dirty footprints on the windowsill when he goes in through your window."

Laughing, I asked, "You knew about that?"

She scoffed. "Of course I did. Every time he *snuck in,* we were aware of it. You two weren't nearly as quiet as you thought you were. We didn't bust you because you weren't doing anything nefarious."

I laughed again.

After trying the dress on with the shoes and my new jewelry, I spun in a circle with a giddy laugh and smile. It was perfect!

"I think you're going to get at least three courting proposals tomorrow in that dress," Mom said with a nod.

"Have you received proposals for me?" It wasn't uncommon for parents to send in proposals to royals to try to convince them to set up blind dates for an eligible royal.

"Yes, a few over the years, but we turned them all down."

"Why?" I asked as I stripped out of the dress.

"Because if you wanted a blind date, you would have told us. We figured you weren't ready to court yet and that you would let us know when you were ready. Plus, you were still in college."

"I'm definitely ready now," I said with a nod. Butterflies swirled in my stomach at the thought of potentially courting Kayden, Trey, and Mason. They were a packaged deal, after all.

"Good to know. I'll make sure to make a list of those who request to be added to potential suitors." She smiled and winked at me.

"Is there anything else we need to do to prepare for tomorrow?" I asked as we walked to the car.

"No, everything else is all ready!"

"Great, that means I can get a good night's sleep in preparation for the storm tomorrow."

"Good luck with that," she said, and laughed.

SEVEN

Hair, makeup, and getting dressed took over three hours, the longest I'd ever taken to get ready. Mom had insisted I wear my tiara, so I'd had to change my hair plans, which made the stylist have to change their original idea.

My nerves grew as I stared at my reflection. My hair was glowing faintly, but I was keeping the rage at bay without much issue.

"You look amazing!" Maya gasped and walked around me with her mouth open. "That dress is so sexy! Oh, man. The guys are going to be on you like ants on sugar."

Chuckling, I hugged her. "Your dress is amazing, too." It was white with red rhinestones in a swirling pattern from her cleavage around her waist and down her legs. "I think you might steal all the single men's attention instead."

She flipped her hair over her shoulder and posed next to me in front of the mirror. "We can steal all the attention and then have our pick of men."

I hadn't told her about what had happened yesterday, still in shock and disbelief myself.

"Well, let's hope there are some handsome, eligible men for us tonight," I said.

"It's time!" Mom called as she entered the room. Her hands went up to her mouth as tears built in her eyes. "Oh, honey, you look amazing!" She hugged me and kissed my cheek, then turned to Maya. "You look amazing as well!"

"Thanks, Mom Two," Maya said. "Did you see any handsome men out there?"

"Besides my mates? There were a few younger ones," she teased. "Come on, let's get you announced so you can start enjoying your party!" She grabbed Maya and pulled her through the door leading to the huge ballroom, leaving it cracked so I could hear the DJ announce my entrance.

Taking a deep breath, I smoothed down my dress, reminded myself this was my party and would be fun, and stepped through the door while smiling wide.

Everyone clapped and cheered as I entered and I was immediately hugged and wished happy birthday by all the people inside. In addition to my family and friends, there were family friends, and friends of my parents and grandparents as well. Definitely over one hundred people, but if I counted how many were there, I might get too nervous, so it was better to just focus on the ones that were closest to me. There were several people I didn't recognize, but I greeted everyone like I knew them, just in case they were important people I had met before and forgot.

"Happy birthday, gorgeous!" Luca said as I made it to

him. He kissed my cheek and whispered in my ear, "I'll give you your gift later, after you've made your rounds."

Pulling back, I continued to smile and said, "Thanks for coming, Luca." He was a handsome alpha, with long, light brown wavy hair and light green eyes complimented by a sharp jawline. He was handsome enough to be a model if he wanted to.

"Anything for you, Lily," he said and winked at me.

As attractive as he was, I just never viewed him as a potential mate. His attitude was too cocky at times and it irked me to see him treat those weaker than him as less just because they weren't as strong. He wasn't rude all the time or anything like that, but I'd seen him on occasion be rude to servers or people who tried to interact with him.

People had started dancing and before I realized what was happening, Trey pulled me into a dance, spinning us around the room. "Happy birthday, Lily."

"Thanks, Trey," I said and swallowed nervously.

We had learned the dance together when we were growing up, classical dances were something that our parents required us to learn and since we were all around the same age, Kayden was the youngest by four years, we had practiced together.

"So, now that you know we aren't complete assholes," he said, "why are you talking to guys like that loser?"

I glanced in the direction he was looking, knowing he meant Luca. "He's not a loser. I know him from college. Why would I not talk to him or interact with him? It's not like he has asked to court me or anything."

He frowned. "Is that it? You want to be courted?"

Rolling my eyes, I said, "Every girl wants to be courted, Trey."

"I'm sorry we didn't come see you, but I had been informed that you were in a relationship and knew I couldn't bring Kay or Mas to find you snuggled up with a man without them trying to murder him."

"What are you talking about?" I asked, stopping dancing to look at him.

He pulled me back into the dancers spinning around the room. "I had someone follow you for a bit at the college after you blocked our numbers. About a month after, they said you were spending a lot of time with that guy." He jerked his chin towards Luca as we passed him again.

I threw my head back as I laughed and shook my head.

"Wait," I said, realizing something. "I didn't block your number. I only blocked Kayden's. You were the one who stopped calling and texting me."

"My calls, and Mason's, were blocked as well. I bet if you check your phone, you will find that all are blocked."

"Mind if I cut in?" Mason asked just as the song ended, before I could respond to Trey's claims.

Trey's hand gripped me tighter a second, clearly not wanting to end the conversation yet. But, after a moment, he bowed to me, holding my hand still, and kissed the back of it before transferring my hand to Mason's outstretched palm.

The next song started and Mason expertly spun us around the room. He was the quiet, brooding alpha, the one who many considered a loose cannon because he often reacted swiftly with violence instead of trying to talk things out. There were some who thought he was wild and untamable, a threat more than a protector. His dark hair was shorter than the last time I had seen him, shaved on the sides and a few inches long on the top, so it hung in stylish waves that were all natural. His blackish-blue hair was the same color as his raven wings in animal form.

"Happy birthday," he said after a silent minute of dancing.

"Thank you," I replied and gave him a tense smile.

"You look gorgeous," he added, his eyes dipping to my cleavage before he averted his gaze, making me smile truly.

"You look good in the suit," I said.

He grunted. "I only wore it so you would be less embarrassed to dance with me."

My brows furrowed. "Why would I be embarrassed to dance with you?"

"You know, plus if I just wore slacks and a shirt, we would stand out more than usual," he explained.

"I've never been embarrassed to be seen with you," I said honestly.

His eyes snapped to mine and widened a bit as he realized I was being sincere. "I ..." he paused, looked around as if making sure no one could hear us, then leaned closer to whisper, "... I missed you."

Emotional vulnerability was so hard for him. Had anyone else spoken in such a way, I would have laughed, but laughing would hurt his feelings and make him shut down.

"You could have come to see me," I said softly, sadly.

He shook his head. "I might have killed someone."

That wildness people worried about wasn't too far off at times. "It would have helped mend our ... issues."

His brows furrowed. "You really thought we didn't care for you?"

My throat constricted and instead of responding verbally, I nodded.

His grip on my hip tightened and his eyes softened. "I'm sorry, Lily. I tried to convince Trey to go see you, but he wouldn't and wouldn't tell me why he wouldn't let us. You know he never gives orders, but he straight forbade us from going."

If he'd told Mason that he had heard I was dating someone, I wasn't sure what Mason would have done, knowing he was interested in me.

As we danced, I allowed myself to enjoy his presence, something I'd loved as a child, but had missed so much the past few years. He had been a constant in my life and being without him as well as Trey and Kayden while so far away from my family had made it even harder. I was proud of myself for enduring it and graduating, but it was so nice to be able to smell him and touch him. His wildness, his darkness, was similar to mine and I'd always felt like we were meant to find each other, though I'd never admitted that to anyone. The urge to rest my head on his shoulder was intense, but I resisted as the reminder of the pain of being separated was still fresh.

The song ended and Mason stopped, staring down at me. "Lily, I know we messed up. I know we hurt you. I'm sorry. Will you go with me somewhere tomorrow?"

Was he asking me on a date? Or was he going to show me something? "What time?" I asked.

"My turn to dance with the beautiful princess," Luca said, grabbed my hand, and pulled me away from Mason.

Mason growled and took a step towards us, but Trey put a hand on Mason's chest and shook his head.

Luca smiled at me as we danced, completely oblivious to the danger he was in with that stunt. "It's rare now to find women who have been trained with classical dances. I don't often get to show my skills." He spun me in a circle so fast I got dizzy for a second, then slid his arm around my back to pull me close. "So, Princess, I spoke with your mother and requested a chance to court you."

"Oh, uh, that's quite a compliment," I said and laughed awkwardly. "I didn't think you were the type of guy to settle down."

He spun me again, but I was prepared this time so I didn't trip or get dizzy. Bending down, he whispered in my ear, "For the right woman, I'll do almost anything. Even stop my playboy ways."

Why did that sound like a lie?

"Mind if I cut in?" Kayden asked and pulled me by the waist away from Luca.

"Um, I do mind, actually," Luca said and tried to follow us, but Trey stepped in front of Luca, introducing himself and stopping him.

"Happy birthday," Kayden said. His thumb rubbed my side where it rested on my hip.

"Thank you for making an appearance," I replied. "I know you hate dressing up."

"Mason grumbled the entire way here." He laughed and shook his head.

The song ended and he bent close to whisper in my ear, "A gift is on your bed." His lips pressed gently against my cheek before he turned and walked away, leaving me hot and breathing uneven.

"Time for cake," Maya said and looped her arm through mine as she pulled me towards a huge cake on a table at the end of the room. Leaning close, she whispered, "The trio were looking at you much differently than when we were kids. And that other alpha was definitely interested as well."

"I'm definitely not interested in him," I said, ignoring her comment about the trio.

The DJ made the announcement that we were cutting the cake and everyone turned to watch as I walked up and took the knife from Mom.

"Not a word," I said out of the side of my mouth to her when I saw her smirk.

"I've got a list of ten names already," she said, "and it's only been two hours."

"I don't want to know right now, let's discuss that tomorrow," I said and shook my head.

"Look this way!" a photographer said and began snapping pictures of Mom and I as I cut the cake.

The rest of the night was spent dancing with family and a few guys I had never met before that I highly suspected were invited by my grandparents and great grandparents.

I stepped outside for some fresh air and gasped as a pair of gloved hands grabbed me around the face. Spinning in the hold, I pushed the attacker away as hard as I could, causing them to fly into the wall.

It was a man I'd never seen before with a huge scar down his face and a pair of black gloves on his hands.

"Who are you and what do you want?" I demanded, arms up in preparation to fight.

He didn't respond, just snarled, shifted into a werewolf warrior form, and attacked me again. His claws cut through the tips of his gloves and scratched my face, causing little rivulets of blood to drip down my cheek.

"Lily!" Maya screamed and ran outside, calling her fire to coat her hands as she started attacking the man, keeping him away from me.

Her scream had alerted those inside and Mason and Kayden immediately ran outside.

The man jumped over the railing as soon as he saw them, fleeing.

"Go!" Trey snapped at Mason and Kayden. Both jumped over the railing and followed after the attacker. Trey set his hands on my shoulders, looking at my scratched face. "Are you alright?"

I nodded.

"What's going on?" Grandpa Deryn, King of the Were-wolves, asked as my family came out. Great Grandpa Dan right behind him.

"A werewolf attacked me," I said. "He had a large scar down his face, on the left side, and could take a warrior form."

Grandpa Deryn growled, turned to Ezio as he came out, and said, "I want him brought to me *alive*." Grandpa Deryn and my other grandfathers had recently taken over their places as kings of their clans. My great grandparents were still involved, but in a much less significant capacity, trying to enjoy retirement.

Ezio nodded and leapt over the railing to go after them and keep Mason and Kayden from killing my attacker.

Smiling, I turned to everyone and said, "Let's go back and enjoy the party! What's a royal party without an attempted assassination, am I right?"

Several people laughed, but my family looked at each other questioningly. Why was I attacked now when I'd been safe the entire time at the college? I had never had something like this happen before. Who could have sent them? Or why did they decide to come after me?

People went back inside and the party resumed, but Caleb walked over and set his hand on top of my head. "We'll find out what prompted this, don't worry, cub."

I knew as a hybrid that I was viewed as less than other races and there were still some who wished they could eradicate us, but it had been decades since we'd had issues like this.

Trey followed behind me as I went back inside and up to the bar.

While I ordered a drink, he grabbed a napkin, poured water over it, and started cleaning my cheek. Since I had shapeshifter healing, the scratches were healed, but the blood had remained.

"Thanks," I whispered as I held still for him to finish cleaning the blood. He wiped a bit off my shoulder where it had dripped as well.

Reaching out for the glass of sparkling wine, I scowled at my shaking hand. Why was I shaking? I wasn't scared.

Trey stepped closer to me, dropped his head down, and said, "We will find out who did this and why, and we won't let anyone else harm you."

Tilting my head back to look at him, I said, "I don't need protection. I'm capable of protecting myself."

"I know you aren't a damsel in distress, Lily."

For some reason him telling me he was going to protect me irritated me, even if he acknowledged I wasn't a damsel in need of saving. "You don't know anything about me from the past four years," I countered and stepped back from him. "You have no idea what I'm capable of."

Grabbing my drink, I spun around, headed away from him, and went back to mingle with strangers. At least with strangers, I could put on a smile and chat the night away.

At least with strangers, I didn't have a painful pressure in my chest when I looked at them.

CHAPTER
EIGHT

"Brunch is ready," Branson said, waking me from where I had passed out on the couch after we got home last night, or more accurately, early this morning.

"Five more minutes," I mumbled.

"It's two o'clock in the afternoon," he said with a chuckle. "You need to get up and rehydrate to help with your hangover."

"Aren't shapeshifters supposed to *not* get hangovers?" I asked as I sat up and immediately gripped my head as it throbbed.

"You're dehydrated, Lily. Drink this." He held out a glass of yellowish water, which meant it had an electrolyte mix in it.

I downed it in two gulps, almost immediately feeling better. "Thanks."

"Some greasy food will help, too," he said and pointed towards the table where Mom, Caleb, and Riddick were eating.

Stumbling over, I took a seat between Riddick and Mom, mumbling, "Morning," to them as I sat.

"We were just going over the list of those who requested to court you," Riddick said.

Groaning, I picked up a breakfast taco. "It's too early for this."

"That alpha you went to college with was very adamant we consider him," Mom said and rested her chin on her joined hands, elbows atop the table. "Something happen at college we need to do know about?"

I scoffed. "Definitely nothing happened. He's a playboy and doesn't realize I can scent his lies."

Caleb's eyes widened. "You can what?"

I flinched, remembering that I hadn't told them about that power or some of my newer powers. "Um, yeah, I can tell when people lie."

"When did that start?" Mom asked.

"Um, when I was fourteen, I think?"

"What?" Caleb, Riddick, and Branson shouted.

My hands flew up to my ears to cover them. "So loud."

"Prove it," Riddick said.

Sighing, I took a huge bite of food and waved my hand at him. "Say two things that are true and one that's a lie. Things I wouldn't know."

He thought a moment and said, "I've seen Caleb cry. I stole a bottle of alcohol from a store. I have never eaten a peach."

My eyes widened. "How have you never eaten a peach?"

"What was the lie?" he asked instead of answering.

"The bottle of alcohol," I answered. "Now, why haven't you eaten a peach?"

"The fuzzy outside grosses me out," he answered.

"What other powers haven't you told us about?" Caleb asked, eyes narrowed.

Looking down at my plate, I pushed the eggs that had fallen out of my taco around. "Well, um, I can sense lies, see auras most of the time though it is finnicky, and some other powers that just happen randomly."

"Like?" Mom prompted.

"Telepathy, telekinesis, and ... premonitions." There were a couple others, but I kept those to myself.

"Premonitions? You see the future?" Mom asked.

"Sometimes."

"How far in advance?" Caleb asked.

"It varies." I shrugged. "Minutes. Hours." In a whisper I added, "A year."

"Run that back again," Branson said. "A year?"

Sighing, I admitted, "I dreamed about that man attacking me last year."

"That's why you didn't freak out," Mom realized.

"You knew you wouldn't get hurt," Caleb said.

"I knew he would scratch me and that Mason and Kayden would come out and scare him away," I admitted. "I thought it was just a dream until last night."

They all looked at each other silently, giving me time to eat. Finished with my food, I stood, carried the plate to the sink, and said, "I'm going to shower."

"We aren't done talking about this," Mom called out.

"Let's table the discussion for now," I called back as I climbed up the stairs.

I paused inside of my door, seeing a black velvet box and a black envelope on my bed. Kayden had said he'd put a gift on my bed last night. Walking in slowly, I opened the envelope and pulled out the card, snorting at the cartoon snake wearing a party hat. Brats. Opening the card, I blinked at the handwritten note that said:

"Prince Trey of the Dragons, Mason of the Hybrids, and Kayden of the Hybrids officially request to court Princess Liliana of the Hybrids. Please accept this first of many courting gifts."

So, their comments last night had just been confirmation that their plan was correct? Setting the card down, I opened the box, gasping at the gorgeous necklace inside that had a strange power radiating from it.

"So pretty," I whispered and stroked a finger down the bright gem. A warm feeling spread through me as I touched it. Setting it down, I went to shower and change before I returned to it, put it on, and looked in the mirror.

"I knew you would like it," Kayden said from my windowsill.

Screaming, I turned, realized who it was, and hissed at him.

He sat down on the windowsill, one leg bent, and rested his arm atop the knee with a smirk. "You need to be more aware of your surroundings."

"Kayden! Stop using the damn window!" Mom yelled from downstairs.

His eyes widened and he dropped his leg. "She knew?" he whispered.

"She's known since we were kids, apparently." I rolled my eyes. "Why didn't you use the front door anyway? You know everyone's home."

"I was hoping to scare you," he admitted with a wide, mischievous smile that reminded me of the boy I used to know.

"Come on, let's go downstairs before my dads come up here and throw a fit," I said as I pulled open my door.

He grabbed my hand, stopping me, and asked, "Are you busy today?"

"I was asked out on a date today, actually," I said.

He growled. "By who? That dragon douche?"

"No," I said, but didn't say who it was.

"What are you doing tomorrow?" he asked, still growling softly.

Pulling my hand free from his grasp, I walked down the stairs and he followed. "I don't think I have any plans. Why?"

"Would you go—"

Someone knocked on the front door twice before pushing it open and stepping inside.

Mason and Kayden tensed as their eyes connected.

"Let's go over the courting request list," Mom said as she walked in, but froze when she saw Mason and Kayden. "Oh, uh, hi, boys."

"List?" Mason asked. "As in more than us?" He walked over and peered over her shoulder at the list, eyes widening when he saw it.

He tried to take it, but she spun away and pulled the list out of his reach.

"Bad!" she snapped at him and shook her finger like he was still a child as he tried to grab it yet again. He forced her to move around the couch, out of his reach, but continued to follow her, eyes focused on the paper.

"You should just burn that list," Kayden said and folded his arms over his chest.

Mason nodded his agreement.

Branson walked in and glared at Mason. "Why are you stalking my mate?"

"I want that list," Mason said and pointed.

"What are you going to do with it?" Branson asked and arched a brow.

"Convince them they don't want to go down this path," Mason said. "That their life will be much better if they stay away from Lily."

"Are you saying being with me is a curse?" I asked with a scowl and put my hands on my hips.

"Of course not," he said and tried to go around Branson, but Branson put his arm out and growled at him.

Mom sat down on the couch and I walked over to sit beside her, leaning my chin on her shoulder while looking at the list, I gasped at the names there. "Did you add some names on your own?"

She shook her head. "They all came up to me last night."

"Liar," I accused even though I knew she wasn't.

She just looked at me with a knowing expression.

I pointed at a name on the list. "Him?"

"Who?" Kayden asked, coming to stand behind the couch.

"Prince Liam of the Elves," Mom answered and smirked when I turned and glared at her.

Kayden's eyes widened. "I didn't realize you were friends with him."

"I'm not," I replied.

"She can be courted by those she hasn't even met before. She doesn't need to know them yet. That's the point of courting. To get to know each other and see if you're a good fit," Mom answered. "Her list would be far too short if it was just people she'd been friends with previously."

Mason growled. "She's wearing our gift."

Mom's eyes dipped to the necklace and I reached up to touch it.

"A courting gift?" she asked.

"Yes," Mason and Kayden said simultaneously.

"Apparently I don't get a birthday gift," I said and sighed dramatically. "I feel a bit unappreciated and unloved. My childhood friends didn't get me a birthday gift, but stole my first dances."

"Oh, you do have some gifts in the car," Mom said and perked up. Looking over her shoulder at Riddick and Caleb at the dining table, she asked, "Can you go bring them in, please?"

They got up and Branson, after pointing at Mason with a glare to behave, went out to help as well.

"Are you really thinking about letting others court you?" Kayden asked, and sat on the couch opposite us.

"You don't get to return after being away from her for years and demand she only courts you," Mom said sternly.

"We made a promise," Mason said as he sat by Kayden.

"Your childhood mating promise?" Mom asked with a scowl as she looked between us.

"You knew about that?" I asked, my mouth hanging open.

"Yes. You came home and told me about it," she said with a soft laugh. "Made me promise not to tell your dads."

"What did you promise not to tell us?" Caleb asked as he reentered carrying tons of bags in his hands. "I thought we told each other everything."

"Let's not talk about this anymore," Mason said. "I came to pick Lily up. She agreed to go with me today."

"I don't care about your promise. She deserves to be courted, to find the mate, or mates, who will treat her well and love her the best. So, I'm vetoing your promise as it is not legally binding since you were all children," Mom said sternly.

They frowned, but stayed quiet.

"I want to open my gifts before I leave," I told Mason. "You didn't tell me what time you were coming, so I'm not ready to go anywhere, and you didn't tell me where we're going, so I don't know what to wear."

"What you're wearing is fine," he said. "It really doesn't matter what you wear."

They set all the bags and boxes on the table in front of me and I grabbed the nearest one, reading the card before I opened the gift.

Kayden picked one up and snarled.

Assuming it was from Luca, I grabbed it from him before

he broke it or something, and opened it. A pair of beautiful ruby earrings that matched my eyes when I was in snake form, dangled in a small box. There was also an envelope with a hotel key inside to one of the nicest hotels in the city.

"Whoa, that's ... bold," Mom said with a soft laugh.

Sighing, I shook my head. "I am honestly not surprised."

"Can I cross him off your courting list?" she asked.

"Yes," all of my dads present said at the same time as Mason and Kayden.

"Do you want me to set up the dates?" Mom asked, ignoring them all. "Are there any you want to mark off?"

"Yes," I said and pointed at three names. "They have made periodic anti-hybrid comments. I think their parents put them up to asking to court me."

She scribbled their names out aggressively.

"I haven't heard anything good about this guy," Branson said and pointed at a name on the list. "He's an aggressive werewolf with bad views about women."

Mom scribbled his name off just as aggressively as the others.

"Not him either," Riddick said, pointing at a name I didn't recognize. "He's an asshole."

"He's gay," Caleb said and pointed at one of the names. "I'm pretty sure his grandpa made him submit his name."

"Let's set up a date with him," I said as I picked up the next gift to open. "That way his grandpa won't have any reason to be upset with him."

Mom nodded. "He'll be my first call."

"Who's your second call?" Caleb asked.

"Prince Liam," she answered immediately.

"This is all pointless," Kayden growled.

"Scared of a little competition?" Caleb asked with a smirk.

I loved my adoptive dad a lot, but it was times like this that I absolutely adored him and his confidence.

Kayden scoffed and rolled his eyes. "Those males couldn't last a second with us."

He shrugged. "Prove it then. Win her heart by courting her. You think your promise is all that matters, but what matters is that she finds mates who genuinely care about and love her and are capable of providing her the life she deserves. We know you can protect her physically, but can you win her heart again, and prove you can protect it?"

Mason and Kayden were quiet after that, watching as I opened more gifts. After about five minutes, Mason stood and asked, "Can you be ready in thirty minutes to go on a shopping trip with me?"

A shopping trip? He hated shopping.

"Sure," I agreed with a nod.

He nodded back and walked out of the house.

Kayden frowned at the door then looked at Mom and I. "Are you available tomorrow evening to go on a date?"

"What time?" Mom asked.

"Six?" he asked back.

She pulled out a small calendar book from a bag on the floor and wrote in it as she nodded. "Done."

He bowed to me. "See you tomorrow, Princess."

When the door shut behind him, Caleb said, "Things are about to get interesting around here! Finally!"

"I'll make the calls, get stuff scheduled, and put this calendar on your desk in your room, okay?" Mom said.

Laughing, I asked, "You purchased that calendar just for this, didn't you?"

"I already had it," she admitted, "and it seemed like the perfect reason to use it."

I laughed, stood, and asked, "Can you help me carry this stuff up to my room? I want to change before Mason comes back."

"Make them fight for you," Caleb said and set his hand on my shoulder. "I know you guys have a history, but I meant what I said. You deserve to be wined and dined like every other woman."

Hopping up, I kissed his cheek. "Thanks, Dad."

Loading our hands and arms up, we all carried the gifts up the stairs and to my room, spreading them out on the floor. I opened all the envelopes, knowing those would have cash and gift cards, and put them inside of my purse.

Hurrying, I changed into a nicer shirt, brushed out my hair, and put some makeup on. Just as I finished, I heard the front door open.

Rushing downstairs with my purse on my shoulder and my shoes in my hands, I smiled at Mason. "I'm ready!"

He looked at my shoes and said, "Almost."

I hopped on one foot as I put one shoe on and then the other. "Okay, now I'm ready."

"Have fun!" Mom yelled from the kitchen.

"Remember, I know where you live!" Caleb yelled as we walked out.

"That's probably the scariest threat I've ever received," Mason mumbled.

CHAPTER
NINE

Ezio smiled at me from the driver's seat as I climbed into the back of the SUV. "Good afternoon. How are you feeling?"

"Good. How are you today?" I asked as I buckled.

Mason sat beside me, buckling his belt as well.

"Good. You ready?"

"Yes," Mason replied.

Ezio nodded and put the vehicle into gear, driving through the gate.

We drove in silence, Mason looking out his window the entire time. I opened my mouth a couple of times to try to start a conversation, but decided to stay silent instead. He was supposed to be courting me and if he didn't have anything to say, then I'd just stay quiet.

He had often been quiet when we were kids, too, so it wasn't completely abnormal. Mason was definitely someone who proved his feelings by actions instead of flowery words or speeches.

Glancing at him, I took in the worn jeans, tight black t-shirt, and noticed a bit of black on his collarbone peeking out from the shirt. Did he have a tattoo? He hadn't had any last time I saw him.

Ezio parked in the garage at the mall and said, "I'll stay as far back as I can while also being close enough should danger show up."

"She'll be safe with me," Mason said with certainty and held open the door for me to climb out.

We walked through the automatic doors and I tried to let Mason lead, but he stayed at my side.

"So, what are we here to buy?" I asked and looked over at him.

He had his hands in his pockets and glanced away with pink on his cheeks. "Your birthday present."

My eyes widened. "My birthday present?"

He nodded and said, "I'm not the best present buyer in general and I have no idea what things you have or don't have already. Plus, it's been a while since we talked, so I don't know if your tastes have changed." He turned to me. "Is this okay?"

It was incredibly sweet of him to have thought of this and to be willing to go with me knowing I could shop for hours. His gift wasn't going to be just what he bought me, but the time he spent with me. He really had grown a lot the last few years.

I nodded and smiled at him. "Yeah. This is okay."

The first store we came to was a dress store. I walked inside and headed towards the clearance rack.

"I have money," he said. "You don't need to buy from the clearance side."

"I like looking at the dresses here first," I explained. "Sometimes you can find really cute things and save money at the same time." Pulling two dresses off the rack, I headed over to another display to look at a pretty off-white dress I'd seen.

"This one would look really good on you," he said and held up a black mermaid cut, velvet dress.

I checked the size and took it from him. "That's a really pretty one."

His lip twitched in a smile and he moved to another rack to look for more dresses to offer me. By the time I made it to the dressing room, I had ten dresses to try on.

The two women who had been at the dressing room hurried away when Mason got close, his alpha presence and scowl enough to scare them away.

"How have you been, Mas?" I asked as I closed the curtain between us and stripped out of my clothes, slipping the first clearance dress I'd found on.

"Fine," he replied gruffly.

"Come on, give me more than that," I said with a soft laugh. "It's been years. Tell me something."

"I've been fine. The demon hunting keeps us busy enough that I don't have too much free time. What free time I do have, I usually spend training and occasionally doing fun things the others force me to do. I did a few jobs for King Deryn and King Nico."

"Do you enjoy demon hunting?" I asked as I struggled with the zipper. Finally getting it zipped up, I pushed the curtain aside so I could step out.

"I do," Mason answered. "It's simple and an outlet for my anger." He had been looking at the ceiling, his arms spread across the back of the couch, but he lowered his head when I stepped out. "The color doesn't look as complimentary as I thought, but the style suits you," he commented.

I nodded. "That was my thought as well." Mason was one person who would give me a one hundred percent honest reaction.

Going back inside the dressing room, I tried on one of the other dresses, but didn't like how it looked, so I switched to another one.

When I stepped out Mason said, "That's nice, but not as nice as the first one."

"I'll put it in the maybe pile," I said as I stepped back and closed the curtain to try on another dress.

Two more both with meh reactions.

Looking at the next options, I decided to try on the mermaid style dress he had chosen and threw open the curtain again.

His eyes widened, his arms fell from the back of the couch, and he leaned forward, licking his lips. "That looks even better than I imagined."

Doing a small spin I asked, "So, you think I should get it?"

He nodded. "Yes."

"Let me check the price first," I said.

"Doesn't matter. Get it," he said immediately.

When I turned to head back in, I looked back out of the corner of my eye and caught him taking a picture of me with his phone.

Smirking, I closed the curtain, then waited a moment and said, "Mas?"

"Yeah?"

"Can you help me with the zipper? I can't get it."

With zero hesitation, he stepped inside, closed the curtain behind him, and started to unzip it. His fingers stroked my bare skin, making goosebumps rise and causing me to suck in a sharp breath. My hair began to glow a bit, lighting up the room, and stirring the darkness within me.

Mason's aura changed slightly, the darkness bleeding into a red and black smoke around him. He looked down at me, his eyes darting to my lips before going back to my eyes. "Good?"

Turning to face him fully, I asked, "Did you really miss me or just the familiarity of home?"

Leaning forward, he drew in a deep, loud breath, and his body shuddered. "You." Zero hint of lie.

Tilting my head back, I moved so our mouths were closer and asked, "What would you do if I kissed you right now, Mason?"

"Why don't you find out?" he asked and leaned down closer, caging me in with his body. Most would have been terrified to have him caging them in like this, but it only made my hair glow brighter and my lower body tighten as need coursed through me.

I had kissed Mason twice when we were teenagers and both were kisses I would never forget. A hungry, all-consuming kiss that had branded my soul. Would it feel like that again?

Closing the distance, I pressed my lips to his.

He walked in more, forcing me to back up until my back pressed against the cold glass, and put his hand on the glass next to my face as he kissed me back, his tongue flicking out along the seam of my lips.

I opened my mouth and he made a chirp of satisfaction in his throat before sliding a hand along the back of my neck, pulling me close, and devoured my mouth, his tongue sweeping inside and stroking along mine.

A whimper escaped me and he jerked back like I'd electrocuted him. "Sorry," he panted and started to leave, but I grabbed his hand, stopping him.

"Where are you going?" I asked, panting heavily.

"You whimpered," he whispered, pain edging his words.

"That wasn't a scared or hurt whimper," I explained. "Come back."

He looked down at me with a frown. "It wasn't?"

I shook my head. "It wasn't." I pulled his head down and kissed him again.

He melted against me, picked me up by the butt, and pressed me against the wall of the dressing room, his mouth moved down to kiss and licked at my neck.

"I missed you so much, Lily," he whispered against my neck as he kissed and nibbled. "I dreamed of kissing you again so many times. I wanted to kiss you so many times before we left to start hunting demons, but I was too afraid. I won't let that fear rule me when it comes to you ever again."

Words failed me, so I kissed him again.

"Do you need help with a dress?" an employee asked outside the dressing room.

Jerking away from Mason, my face flushing in embarrassment, I said, "No, I'm good, thanks."

Mason set me down, smiled wide, and waited until she

walked away before he said, "I think they wanted to make sure we didn't have sex in here."

I nodded and looked down, too embarrassed to look at him more. "Seems that way."

He chuckled. "Lucky for them, I refuse to let our first time be in a dressing room."

"You have our first time planned already?" I asked and smoothed my hair down. "That's a bit cocky, don't you think?"

His warm lips pressed against my ear as he said, "The only thing cocky here is you thinking I won't absolutely destroy anyone who gets between you and I. I'll follow along with your courting request, Lily, but you are mine, have been since I was six years old, and it's only a matter of you accepting that. Once you do, I'm going to show you exactly what my plan is for this sexy, delicious body of yours." He inhaled deeply and said, "Though, perhaps a little taste won't be bad."

My brows furrowed, unsure what he meant.

Dropping to his knees, he pushed the dress up to my waist, pushed my knee to spread my legs, and leaned forward, licking me through my underwear.

I gasped and leaned my upper back against the glass, finding the coldness soothing as the rest of my body was burning hot. It wasn't enough though, so I pulled the dress off completely, uncaring that he was going to see me in my thong and bra.

Slipping his finger beneath my thong, he pulled the cloth to the side, exposing my drenched core.

"Seems I'm not the only one who wanted a taste today,"

he said, leaned forward, and licked between my folds. He groaned softly and licked me again.

Leaning my head back against the glass, I panted softly, trying to ensure I didn't make enough noise the employees would hear me.

Mason sucked on my clit, making me gasp, and swirled his tongue around it, sending electric zings through me.

Looking down at him, I caught him looking up at me while he began doing something with his tongue that sent me right over the edge. The darkness in his aura swirled around him, mingling with mine, connected.

I bit my lip to keep from crying out as my body shuddered, my legs shook, and stars danced across my vision. I tried to move away, but he pressed a hand to my stomach, holding me in place as he continued to lick me, making me ride out the orgasm fully.

Standing, a satisfied smile on his face, he wiped his mouth with the back of his hand and said, "I'll take these and pay while you get dressed." He grabbed the dress I'd had on and one other, stepped out of the dressing room, and closed the curtain between us.

I slid to the ground, panting, and satisfied for the first time in a long time.

Kissing him like that had not been in the plan and being eaten by him had *definitely* not been in the plan, but there was something about Mason that had always called to me. That dark smokey aura that felt like it was a piece of me.

After getting dressed, I walked out to see him sitting with the bags, still smiling happily. As we went on to the next stores, he walked closer to me, our hands brushing together on occasion.

Tension had eased between us and I felt happy and relaxed, safe with him at my side.

A little girl ran over, a book and pen in her hand. "Princess! Princess!" she shouted.

Mason tensed, but I set a hand on his arm, smiled wide, and dropped down into a squat so I was at her eye level. "Hello."

She moved from foot to foot in excitement. "Can you sign this, please?"

"Certainly," I said with a nod, took the pen and book, and opened it. My eyes widened when I saw Mom's and my dads' signatures all inside. I went to an empty page and signed my name, then drew a cute snake curled around a lily, the same drawing I always did when I gave people autographs. Mom always put a bunny head wearing a crown with her autographs.

The little girl squealed, threw her arms around my neck, and took the book and pen back. "Thank you!" she yelled as she ran back across the walkway, waving to me.

A man bumped into her, knocking her down, and sending her book sliding across the ground.

"Watch where you're going, kid!" the man snapped.

Mason set the bags down and growled as he stalked towards the man with his fists clenched at his sides. He stepped right up into the man's face. "You're the one who should watch where you're going. What kind of man is rude to a child like that?"

Hurrying over, I helped the little girl up and got her book for her. "You okay?" I asked as I dusted her off.

She sniffled as she wiped her face and dusted off her hands. "Yes, I'm sorry."

"Who the fuck are you? Captain-Save-a-Hoe?" the man scoffed at Mason, but I watched his throat bobbed as he swallowed hard.

Shooting up to my feet, I stepped in front of Mason and glared at the man. "Apologize to her right now."

He leered at me. "Well, hello, beautiful. I didn't see you there."

Mason growled and the man took a step back.

Drawing in a breath, I checked his scent ... a dragon shifter.

"I know for a fact that my grandfather would have no qualms with me forcing you to your knees to apologize to that little girl and beg for my forgiveness. In fact, I bet if I called him right now, he'd tell Mason here to teach you some respect."

"Say the word," Mason growled and took a step forward, making the man take another step back.

"Your grandfather?" he asked with a scowl. His eyes darted to my hair, glowing with my anger, and widened. "P-Princess L-Liliana. I didn't know you were back."

"Apologize to her right now!" I snapped. My fury boiled over and my magic snapped out to strike his cheek, raising a welt.

People around us stopped to stare, shocked at my anger and order. A few had their phones out, but I didn't care. Let them share the video of me teaching this male to respect those around him.

He stepped around us and stooped down to look at the girl. "I'm sorry, little one. I apologize for knocking you over." Once he'd apologized, he ran away down the walkway.

"Coward," Mason hissed.

The little girl smiled up at me. "Your hair is pretty."

Taking a deep breath, closing my eyes, and focusing on Mason's nearby scent, I calmed down and resealed my rage. When I opened my eyes again, my hair was only slightly glowing. "Thank you."

Her parents stepped forward tentatively, both bowing to me and averting their eyes.

"Have a nice day, Princess!" the little girl called as her parents ushered her away with fear in their eyes.

The necklace around my neck hummed and the next moment a black portal opened beside us.

"Get back!" Mason ordered me and shoved me in the chest, away from the portal as a giant boar-like creature charged out of it.

My feet slid along the tile from his push and I screamed his name as the boar slammed into him, the boar's head level with his chest.

Ezio ran forward, grabbed me, and pushed me behind him, his cell phone up to his ear as he called for backup.

People screamed and fled in multiple directions away from the portal and the fight, but there wasn't much escape except for them since the hallway was narrow, so most ran into a nearby store.

Mason's muscles bulged in his legs as he pushed against the tile and the boar-demon's head, trying to stop it. His jeans ripped around his quads as he took a warrior shift. His booted feet broke down through the tile at the force he was pushing with, and he finally stopped the boar-demon. The boar-demon turned, looked directly at me, and tried to charge away from Mason and towards me.

"No, you don't!" Mason snarled.

Ezio shifted into his warrior form and growled at the demon-boar as he pushed against its head next to Mason.

Mason drew a sword from his back from a scabbard I hadn't seen – how did he keep it hidden from me? – and sliced the boar-demon's head off.

I exhaled in relief, but the relief was short-lived as two hellhounds jumped out of the portal and both immediately headed towards me. They were the size of a standard dog and covered in thick black quills that hurt to touch.

Shifting into my warrior form, including a tail, I used the tail to whip the two hellhounds away from me and back through the portal. I cringed at the pain from touching their porcupine-like quills with my tail.

Three more creatures, these ones large beasts with bull heads and humanoid bodies, stepped through. Their eyes fixated on me as soon as they stepped out.

"Why are they after me?" I gasped as one reached a large hand to try to grab me.

Mason sliced the distracted creature's head off while Ezio fought the other one. "You're clearly enticing to them just like me."

"Flirting while you're fighting? Quite the talent," I teased as a familiar werewolf ran towards us.

"Oh, I have better talents than this, but you aren't ready

for that yet," he said and winked at me, but immediately had to duck as a bat-like demon flew out of the portal and towards his face.

"Get back," Kayden ordered me as he joined Ezio and Mason in fighting the demons that came out of the portal.

"They're after Lily," Mason informed him.

Kayden's eyes darkened as he glanced at me and back at the creatures. "Why?"

"We don't know," I answered as I backed up farther to give them more room.

One of the bull-headed demon creatures charged into Kayden, pushing him back until he was next to me, then flung his head, sending Kayden flying through the air. The creature tried to grab me, but I ducked under his reach and ran around behind him. Jumping up, I leapt onto his back and wrapped my arm around his throat, shifted, and turned into my snake form to wrap around his entire body, and started to squeeze.

He let out a pained bellow as he fell onto his side. I constricted tighter and tighter, hoping the guys would keep any other creatures away from me.

The creature struggled against me, trying to push against my coils, but I was stronger and after several tense moments, finally killed him.

Uncoiling from around him, I surveyed the scene, finding all of the creatures dead and the portal closed.

Shifting into my human form, I asked, "Is anyone injured?"

Ezio sat on the ground, panting. "No, just not as young as I used to be."

Kayden chuckled and patted his shoulder. "You did pretty good, old man."

Mason walked over to me and put his hands on either side of my face. "Are you injured?"

I smiled. "Nope, I'm perfect."

"Now who's being cocky?" he teased and released me.

I sat down beside Ezio and patted his shoulder. "Looks like you got out of shape while I was gone."

He growled then said, "Maybe a little."

"Thanks for the backup," Mason said to Kayden.

"Any day I get a chance to kill a demon is a good day," he said and bumped his fist against Mason's.

Mason retrieved my bags and held his hand out to me. "Ready?"

I looked at the demon bodies.

"Kayden will handle them," he said, glanced at Kayden who scowled at him, and wiggled his fingers at me. "Come on, our date isn't over yet."

Letting him take my hand and pull me to my feet, I followed him farther into the mall, looking back once over my shoulder at Kayden, who was smiling when I looked back.

Why was he smiling like that?

CHAPTER
TEN

"We'll take two of your specials and two margaritas," Mason ordered after we were seated at one of my favorite restaurants just outside of the mall.

They set a basket of chips and a cup of salsa down and Mason immediately grabbed a chip and dipped it in the salsa.

I stole it from his hand and popped it into my mouth. "Stolen food always tastes better."

He rolled his eyes and got himself another chip.

The waiter brought out our drinks and I clinked mine against his. "To a successful first date."

He smiled and took a drink before saying, "Your snake form is much larger than the last time we saw you."

"Yeah, I seem to continue growing," I said. "From some research I've done, it seems like I should stop growing in the next year or so if the animal and I are the same."

"Interesting," he said as he ate another chip.

"So, what are your plans for the rest of the day?" I asked him.

He shrugged. "My only plan was this date."

"Do you want to go have some fun?" I asked.

"I'm always up for some fun with you," he said with a nod. "What did you have in mind?"

"You'll have to wait and see," I said and danced in my seat at the sight of our food coming. "First, food!"

After we finished our food and met Ezio at the SUV, I whispered the location in Ezio's ear.

He laughed and nodded. "You got it."

We pulled up to an inconspicuous white, rectangular building with no sign over the one door that served as the entrance.

"What is this place?" Mason asked as we climbed out.

"I'm going to stay out here," Ezio said. "Holler if you need me."

I saluted him and pulled open the door. "Welcome to a super fun night you'll never forget, Mason."

He walked inside and his eyes widened when he saw the signs inside announcing the business as a black light indoor miniature golf.

Skipping up to the counter, I put cash down and smiled at the teenage boy working behind the counter. "Two please."

"Y-Y-Yes, Princess. Right away." His eyes were wide as saucers as he tapped on the cash register.

Another teenage boy behind him stepped forward and said, "You're even prettier in person than on TV."

Chuckling, I flipped my hair over my shoulder and said, "Thank you, that's so sweet."

Mason growled softly, and the boy took several steps back with a hard swallow.

"Here's your ch-change," the boy at the cash register said and held out a shaking hand with a few bills.

I took it, careful not to touch him. "Thanks!"

"The clubs are by the door over there," he said and pointed towards the entrance to the course. "And you can pick your colored balls from there as well."

"Thank you," Mason said, put a hand on my lower back, and pushed me towards the main entrance.

Talking softly out of the side of my mouth I asked, "Are you really acting possessive in front of teenagers?"

"I don't care how old they are, I don't like seeing other men drooling over you," he whispered back.

We each grabbed a small golf club and picked out golf balls. I chose blue while Mason picked green.

As soon as we stepped through the entrance, the black-lights started reacting to our clothing and the balls in our hand. The first hole was decorated as a rainbow unicorn that you had to hit the ball into its mouth. Once through the mouth, the ball would roll through the unicorn and it would poop it out into the hole.

"Want to make a bet?" I asked as I set my ball down on the starting point.

"I hate making bets with you," he grumbled. "You and Trey."

"That's because we always win them," I said with a wink.

"Name your stakes," he said with a sigh.

"If I win, you have to spend a day with me in your avian form." He wasn't opposed to his bird form, but he preferred to be in his human form.

He scowled. "I get to shift if you're in danger."

I nodded.

"Fine. If I win, you have to send those earrings back to the dragon douche," he said.

My eyes widened. They really hated Luca. Was it for more than the interactions I'd witnessed? Why give back my gift? They were a birthday gift, not a courting gift.

"Fine," I agreed and held out my hand.

He shook my hand, smiled wide, and waved for me to play. "Ladies first."

I hit the ball, but it bounced off of the side of the unicorn's mouth and back towards me.

Mason put his ball down, hit it, and it sailed straight through the unicorn and into the hole, giving him a hole in one.

My mouth dropped and I said, "Beginner's luck."

After four more tries, I finally got my ball through the unicorn.

The next hole was a dragon themed hole where you had to hit it up the dragon's tail, up and over its back along its spine, and down off its nose into the hole.

Once again, Mason got a hole in one.

"How are you so good at this for your first time?" I asked.

"I never said it was my first time," he replied as he spun the club.

I scowled and asked, "When did you play this?"

"On a double date with Trey, we played and I got obsessed with it afterwards. I played occasionally after that, too."

A painful ping went through my chest. "A double date,

huh?" I asked, trying not to let him see that hearing it upset me. I set my ball down and prepared to try to hit it.

"His mom set him up a few times and he begged Kay and I to go. We took turns going with him," he continued, oblivious to my discomfort.

"Hm," I replied and hit the ball. My hit was too hard and it bounced off the dragon's tail and zoomed right back towards my face.

Mason caught it right before it hit my face and scowled at me. "You okay?"

No. No, I was not okay hearing that they had gone on dates with other women. I hadn't gone on a single date. I hadn't kissed a single person after the last time I had kissed Mason. Not a single guy in college. I knew I was acting crazy, but I couldn't stop my emotions as they swirled higher and higher out of control. As the spell activated and tried to alter my normal emotions further. As the darkness begged for me to break something ... someone.

"Fine," I ground out and tried to snatch the ball from his hand.

"Lily, why are you upset?" he asked.

"I'm not," I lied.

He grabbed a strand of my hair and showed the glowing piece to me. "Liar."

Exhaling harshly, I admitted, "It upset me to hear you went on dates."

He smiled. The jerk smiled. "Ah, I see."

My anger grew and his aura swirled around him, reaching out towards me. "Did you kiss them? Or fuck them?" I asked.

He shrugged. "What's it to you? You cut us off, remember?"

"You know why I cut you off."

"I know why you cut Kayden off, but his comment had nothing to do with me," he countered.

"You're all a packaged deal," I reminded him.

"And yet you only kissed me."

"No," I said and shook my head. "I've kissed each of you."

His brows furrowed. "You kissed them, too? When?"

"When we were younger, before I left for college," I answered.

"That makes Trey's partners even more confusing," he whispered as he looked off, deep in thought.

Partners? As in ... sexual partners?

Hissing at him, I spun around and threw my club on the ground. "I'm going home."

Was I overreacting? Yes, but my darkness when stirred around them seemed to make theirs react and it became like a spiral making me more and more irrationally angry.

Mason snatched my wrist, pulling me back so hard that I stopped and spun around, my hands going up to his chest to keep from falling. He pressed his mouth to mine and rubbed his fingers along my cheek. "These are the only lips I've ever kissed."

My eyes widened. "What?"

He nodded. "Honest."

"I don't want to hear about your guys' conquests. What happened while we weren't talking—"

"Lily," he whispered, "you're acting completely unlike yourself."

Pushing away from him, I turned away so he couldn't see my face and said, "You don't know who I am. I'm not the same girl I was four years ago."

"Did something happen?" he asked.

"Lots of things happened," I replied and headed towards the exit. My powers had changed, grown, and gotten out of control. There had been a time that I had almost killed someone without meaning to. As much as I tried to be the sweet, pretty princess that the public thought I was, there was a darker side. The side from the spell that I couldn't always keep at bay.

"We're not the same either," he said softly.

Taking a deep breath, I closed my eyes, and willed myself to calm down. To stop overreacting. "I'm sorry," I whispered.

His arms wrapped around me and he squeezed. "Come on, let's finish our game so I can win."

"Why do you hate Luca so much?" I asked and picked up my club.

"It's obvious that he's a playboy and yet he is trying to court you, which is unacceptable. He's not good enough for you." Adding so quietly that I didn't think he meant for me to hear, "I don't think there's anyone who's good enough."

I hit my ball and it sailed perfectly along the dragon and into the hole.

We finished playing with no more angry incidents and I lost ... horribly, but I was smiling at the end and so was Mason, which had been my plan all along.

"We should probably head home," Mason said as we headed outside. "There's probably demon hunts to go on."

"You guys have been constantly busy, so why are you staying here?" I asked.

He looked at me like that was a stupid question. "We came to claim our mate, to finalize that promise we made, remember?"

Oh, right.

"I—"

He put his finger over my lips and shook his head. "Your parents are right. We need to prove to you that we're your best choices. And to get to know each other again after being apart for so long."

Opening the back passenger door, he waited until I climbed in before closing my door and getting in on the opposite side.

"You two have fun?" Ezio asked as he started the SUV.

We both nodded.

"Good. Where to now?"

"Home," Mason said. "We have adult responsibilities to get back to."

"Well, you do," I countered. "I'm going to go home and take a nap."

He rolled his eyes at me and a small smile appeared at my teasing.

Our ride home was just as silent as the trip out, but this time it was a more comfortable silence.

He helped me carry my bags of gifts into the house and up to my room. Pausing at my desk, he glared at the calendar book Mom had left there.

"Thanks for today," I said to distract him. "It was fun."

He turned around to face me and said, "Don't forget to send back that douche's earrings."

"I don't see why you're so adamant I send back a birthday gift, but I'll do it." I had already planned to just throw away the hotel key.

"I had fun today and I'd like to do it again. Find an open date on your calendar and add my name to it and text me. Oh, and can you unblock our numbers now?"

Pulling out my cell, I let him watch as I unblocked their numbers, confirming that Trey was right and I had blocked all of them. "Done."

He gave me a full smile, kissed my cheek, and said, "See you later, Lily gator."

Before I could respond, he was jogging out the front door.

That phrase, that silly, childish phrase was the one he'd said to me when we'd said goodbye when I'd gone to college. It was a phrase he only said to me when we were alone, too silly for him to say in front of his friends.

And it made my heart pound to hear again.

Flopping down onto my bed, I smiled up at the ceiling. Even with the demon attack and my emotional outburst and insanity, today had been a great day.

I just hoped the other days were just as awesome.

CHAPTER
ELEVEN

Instead of mailing the earrings and hotel key back to Luca, Bran Bran had demanded to personally deliver them and there was nothing I could say to stop him.

Mom just sighed and shook her head as I tried to convince him otherwise and I'd finally given up, letting him do what he wanted.

After my date with Mason, I went on the date with the gay alpha who had thanked me several times for at least going out once with him and had promised that I could call on him for a favor at any time. He was very sweet and we had a lot of similar tastes in music and movies, so the date had gone by amazingly well.

As I finished applying mascara for my date with Prince Liam, Trey knocked on my bedroom door.

"What's up?" I asked him as I put my makeup away and grabbed my purse. "I've got a date to go to."

"I came to give you your belated birthday present," he

said. "I apologize for the delay." He held out a small black box that looked suspiciously like a jewelry box.

"You guys already gave me a necklace," I reminded him. Though I didn't need to remind him since I was still wearing it. I'd debated taking it off last night, but when I touched it, it had felt warm and familiar and I didn't want to take it off.

"I remember," he said with a smile as his eyes darted down to the necklace. "But that was a courting gift. This is a birthday gift."

Opening the box, I blinked at the ornate brass key inside. "What is it a key to?"

He winked and said, "You'll find out on our date tomorrow. Have a great night, Lily."

He knew I hated surprises. He had no doubt given it to me right before my date with Liam on purpose, to try to distract me. Even as an adult, he was such a brat.

Shoving the bratty prince out of my mind, I focused on the elven prince I was headed to see.

Originally, I was supposed to go out with Kayden tonight, but Liam only had tonight available, so Kayden agreed to reschedule our date.

"I'm off to my date," I announced as I walked out the front door.

"Have fun!" Mom called back.

"Bring back a slice of cheesecake!" Dad called out as I shut the door.

While Mom had called to set up the days and times for the dates, the men were the ones who chose where and what we were doing. Of the ones scheduled so far, ninety percent of them were lunch or dinner dates.

Prince Liam was not an exception. He'd made a reservation at one of the most expensive restaurants in the city, the one with the best cheesecake ever. I had already planned to get Mom a slice, since it was her favorite cheesecake.

I climbed into the back of the SUV and my eyes widened when I found Kayden in the driver's seat. "Where's Ezio?"

"It's been determined that you are, like your mother and grandmother, a magnet for trouble, and that my father is, and I quote my mother, 'too old to deal with all the shenanigans.' So, I'm your assigned guard for the day," Kayden replied, a smug smile on his face.

"No," I said and started to climb out of the car.

"The demons were far too interested in you for us to not notice," Kayden said quickly. "King Caleb has requested I go with you in case more demons show up. I've been studying the demons since I was a child and know the most about them, so I'm your best option."

Growling, I said, "Fine, but you will stay on the far side of the restaurant and will not interrupt us unless my life is in danger. Do you understand?"

He nodded and started the vehicle. "I understand."

It didn't escape my notice that he wore a nice pair of slacks and a button-up, silk shirt with the sleeves rolled up, exposing his forearms. Did he know that was one of my favorite things? Or had he guessed? Or was he just ... naturally sexy? Well, I knew the last question was definitely true.

"Look on the seat beside you," he said after he'd been silent as we drove out of the hybrid clan territory.

Frowning, I looked to my left and my eyes widened at the

117

sight of an envelope with a red bow atop it. How had I not noticed that when I'd climbed in?

Opening it, I pulled out two tickets to a concert in two nights. Front row seats to one of my favorite bands.

"Is this the plan for our date?" I asked, giddy excitement coursing through me that I failed to hide in my higher pitched voice.

He nodded, smiling slightly.

"How did you get tickets like this last minute? They've been sold out for a year." I knew as I'd tried to buy them.

"I have my ways," he answered vaguely. "The rumor is that while you were at college, you didn't do anything fun. I thought we should rectify that."

I *hadn't* done anything fun during college.

"Sounds great," I said and put the tickets back into the envelope.

"How was your date with Mason?" he asked.

"He didn't tell you?" I asked back. When we were younger, they had told each other everything.

"He's been busy since then, so we haven't really had time for idle chit chat."

"Demons?" I asked, worried.

"And other things," he replied vaguely.

Why were the demons showing up so much more often than even five years ago?

"How many variations of demon creatures have you encountered so far?" I asked.

"About one dozen," he answered.

"That's not that many," I whispered and tapped my mouth as I considered the kind I had seen.

"If you are interested in learning more about demons, we have a book which we use to record the information we learn and some drawings as well."

"I would love to read that," I said immediately.

"Come by the house one of the days you're not being courted and we'll show you," he said.

He was totally pulling at my insatiable curiosity, and I was one hundred percent going to fall for it.

"I'll check my schedule," I said and gave him a huge smile in the rearview mirror as he, meeting my expectations, looked back at me with a scowl.

He didn't talk to me the rest of the drive, which was fine because it gave me time to text Maya and apologize for being so busy. She demanded a girls' night, so I sent a message in the group chat I had with Mom, Great Aunt Leona, and Nana Jolie asking for their availability. While they weren't our age, they were a ton of fun to hang out with and always held the best girls' nights.

"We're here," Kayden announced as he put the vehicle in park, got out, and opened the door for me. He held out his hand to help me out, and I accepted with a smile, ignoring the thrill that ran from his fingers up my arm.

After I smoothed down my dress, I straightened my back, and walked into the restaurant.

The host bowed deeply and led the way to the back, to a private room where Liam was already seated. He was handsome, regal-like, and wore a grey suit that was definitely tailored just for him. His long, silver hair was tied back with a silver butterfly clip, exposing his pointed ears.

When he saw me enter, he stood, walked to me, picked

my hand up, and kissed my knuckles. "Good evening, Princess."

"Thank you for your request to dine with me, Prince Liam."

He pulled out my chair and pushed it in as I sat. "Only a fool would waste such a rare opportunity as to get to know the elusive and gorgeous hybrid princess."

Laughing softly, I set my napkin on my lap, and said, "I don't think I'm elusive."

The waiter came to my side and asked, "A drink, Your Highness?"

"Your best sparkling wine, please," I requested, "with two cherries, no stems inside."

"I shall return at once," the waiter said, bowed, and rushed out of the room.

Out of the corner of my eye, I saw Kayden move to a corner near the entrance to the private room, taking his place as guard.

"So, tell me about yourself, please," Liam requested.

"What would you like to know?" I asked. "I'm the adopted daughter of King Caleb and Queen Ember, a hybrid with an animal form of a snake, and I just graduated from college."

He shook his head, eyes full of light. "Not the tidbits the media shares about you. Tell me something about *you*. Something the media wouldn't know."

I hadn't been asked something like that before. Pondering, I said, "I absolutely *hate* onions and asparagus."

He laughed, and the sound was so melodic I swore I

heard bells. "That's definitely not something I expected you to say."

"Tell me about yourself," I said.

Smirking he answered, "I'm a Prince of Elves, third in line for heir, love water skiing, and have an animal form of a sparrow."

A sparrow? How interesting.

"And you're not terrified to be considering mating a snake?" I asked and set my chin on steepled fingers with my elbows resting on the table.

"We are not our animals," he said. "At least, not all the time."

That had been a clever way to get around answering my question. So, I let it lie.

"I saw the demon fight at the mall," he said.

My eyes widened. "There's video of it?"

He nodded. "Someone was videotaping you with the alpha you were shopping with when it happened and captured the entire thing."

Oh, boy. Why hadn't anyone told me?

"Ah, I see," I replied since I didn't know what else to say.

"Your strength in snake form is truly remarkable. And your speed in general. It was impressive to watch you. Most of the elvish women I know would have simply run away in fear."

"Well, you have to remember how I was raised," I reminded him. "I wasn't given the luxury of a quiet life. Aside from my college days." No one knew about the few events that had happened while I was away, since they'd occurred off campus and had not been recorded.

"Which is what makes you so fascinating," he said. "You are beautiful, smart, and humble. You took time to sign the little girl's book and even drew her a little cartoon character."

"It's part of my autograph," I explained.

"So, what is your plan or goal for the future?" he asked. "Aside from finding a mate, obviously."

"To help my parents with their businesses to ensure the financial stability of our clan. That's why I went to school for business administration."

"And will you, like many of your female family members, opt for a multi-partner relationship or will you be monogamous?"

"Honestly, I'm not sure," I admitted. "I've had both monogamous and triads approach me for courting and I can't say I have a preference as of yet."

He leaned back and stared at me silently for a moment. Just long enough for the waiter to return with my drink and take our order.

"I have to ask, why are you interested in me? You have your pick of women, not just because you're a prince, but because you are handsome and kind. Why throw your hat in the ring?"

"I've truthfully had a crush on you since we were teenagers," he admitted. "I went to the same high school as you."

My mouth dropped. "What! How did I not know that?" How had I not noticed another royal at our school? Especially, a handsome one like him?

"I'm two years younger than you," he explained with a smile. "Plus, you always had Prince Trey and his friend around you. So, I assumed you were basically spoken for. When I heard from my mother that you were back from college, single, and looking for a mate, I thought perhaps it was fate or at least a chance for me to try."

Every single word he had said was true. Wow. I had known that keeping Trey and Mason around me in high school was likely the reason I didn't get asked out much, but I hadn't really cared then. I wasn't looking for a mate then. Poor Kayden was too young to go to high school with us, but he'd made up for the age difference by learning to be one of the strongest alphas, able to hold his own with Mason and Trey against almost any partner. My dad still wiped the floor with them, though.

"I appreciate your honesty," I said. "It's ... refreshing."

Our food came and I took the time eating to think about my choices.

Yes, I had feelings for the trio, and while they were back and had explained the misunderstanding, that didn't completely erase the hurt. And, just because we had been friends when we were younger didn't mean we would be great together as adults. They were often traveling all over the world to hunt demons, which left the question of how often would they be with me, and if our goals even aligned.

There were plenty of other mice in the pantry, as Mom liked to say.

Liam was handsome, kind, and more likely to stay close to me. I didn't know enough about him yet or know if there was a connection between us, but there was plenty of time for that.

"What is your goal?" I asked once I'd finished my food.

"I am very unlikely to become king, so I would like to move across the ocean and open a small business there to live a quiet life. Although I may be spoiled currently, I prefer a simplistic life."

"So, this restaurant was because you thought it was something I would prefer?" I asked.

He laughed softly. "Yes, and a way to impress you."

The cheesecake I had ordered to take back to Mom arrived. I stood and said, "It was nice talking to you tonight, Liam. Would you like to do something a bit more interactive next time?"

His eyes widened a moment, but he quickly smiled. "That sounds lovely." He picked my hand up, kissed my knuckles, and said, "I look forward to seeing you again, Lily."

The necklace warmed against my chest and I put a hand up to it, worry causing me to grab the cheesecake box and hurry out past Kayden and out to the street, following the feeling.

"Where are you going? What's wrong? Did he do something?" Kayden fired off the questions so fast I couldn't have even answer if I had wanted to.

Clenching the necklace in my hand, I turned down the next alley, and froze as I saw a black portal.

Kayden cursed and pulled out his phone. "How did you know it was here?"

I felt a pull towards the portal and started to walk towards it.

Kayden pulled me back. "What are you doing? Don't get close to it."

"Have you ever tried to peek through?" I asked curiously, tilting my head as I inspected it.

The black portal was a swirling vortex of smoke.

"Of course not," Kayden growled.

"What if I shift into my snake form and just peek my head through?" I asked, turning to face him. "I can leave ninety percent of my body on this side and you can hold me and pull me back if something happens. I could wrap around your body to help you pull me better."

"Absolutely not! Do you want to die?"

"We don't know that I'd die," I countered and canted my head as I continued to look at the portal. "The demons go back through it."

"What if they don't have oxygen there?" he asked.

"They don't suffocate when they're here, so their atmosphere must be similar."

"There could be one of the bull-men standing on the other side, ready to chop your head off with one of their axes," he snarled.

"Why hasn't anything come through yet?" I asked and peered closer at it.

"Sometimes they open and nothing comes out," he answered.

"Nothing, or something so small you miss it?" I asked him. "How often do you find portals just ... open?"

"Very rarely."

"Is there an average amount of time that it stays open? Do demons get cut in half if they're partially through the portal when it closes?"

"Lily! You are not going through the fucking portal!" he shouted at me, his voice echoing in the alleyway.

The portal closed and the draw disappeared.

"Come on, let's go home," I said and turned around. He thought the conversation was over, but as soon as I was home, I was going to start my own demon researching. Something told me that the key to figuring out what was going on with the demons was only going to be learned by going through one of the portals.

TWELVE

My eyes burned as I continued my demon research. I'd been in front of my computer since I got home from the date, and over fifteen hours later, I was still immersed in it.

There was a lot of information out there, though I knew a lot of it was false or completely fabricated.

I needed to get a look at the book the guys had, but knew Kayden was going to be wary of providing me with it to read now that I had tried to go through the portal.

"Why are you suddenly so interested in demons?" Mason asked from my window.

My scream was short and quickly followed by a sigh. "Why do you all insist on using the window?"

"Going through the front door feels weird," he admitted with a shrug and walked over to stand behind me, leaning over my shoulder to look at the computer screen. "That's all completely wrong."

"Yeah, this site was full of fabricated information," I said and closed it. Spinning in my chair and standing up, I forced him to step back. "Why are you here? I've got a date with Trey tonight."

He nodded. "He sent me to pick you up."

"Pick me up?" I asked with a frown.

"He wants you to come to his house and since you've encountered demons a few times now, he thought it was better if you had an escort."

"Okay, well, give me about ten minutes to get ready," I said and indicated my pajamas. "I'm not dressed yet."

Shrugging, he said, "You look good to me."

When he sat in my chair, my brows rose. "Uh, no. You can't stay here. Go chat with my mom or something."

He spun in the chair, folding his legs up beneath him on the seat. "Why? Are you embarrassed by your underwear or something? I don't care if they're full of holes or have cute little bears on them."

I threw my pillow at his head with a snarl. "I was ten! Bears were cute!"

He caught the pillow while smiling wide. "And so were your undies."

"Get out, Mas!"

He stood, grabbed my waist, and stared down into my eyes. My heart hammered against my chest and it became hard to breathe. "Did you kiss the elf prince yesterday?"

"No," I answered, "not that it's any of your business."

He smiled, released me, and walked out of my room, shutting the door behind him.

What had that been about? Was he just trying to gauge his date against others?

Knowing him, he'd come right back in if I took too long,

so I quickly changed into a cute summer dress that I knew Trey would like, freshened up, and hurried downstairs with a bag that contained my calendar and my demon notes. Hopefully, Kayden hadn't informed Trey or Mason about the demon portal incident and they would let me see the book or, at the very least, answer my demon questions.

Just as I reached the bottom step, I remembered the key Trey had given me and had to run back up to grab it.

Mason sat on the couch, glaring at my mom while she smiled at him.

"Everything okay?" I asked as I slipped my shoes on.

"Peachy," Mom said. "Have fun on your date."

Mason stood and stomped to the door, pulling it open for me.

I glanced at Mom, but she was on her phone messaging someone. Assuming she was just picking on him or teasing him, I followed Mason out and didn't bother asking more.

He drove us just outside the dragon's Den, the dragon's territory where they had their own city, and to the outskirts where Trey's house sat. His parents had purchased it for him when he turned eighteen, though they'd been upset that he had adamantly refused to have his house inside of the Den. It was three stories, had eight bedrooms, and was actually a small, stone castle. He'd even put a catapult and trebuchet on the roof as anti-dragon countermeasures. His mother had *not* appreciated the humor, but his father had.

"You guys use the catapult since you arrived?" I asked.

Mason snorted. "Is Trey breathing?"

He said it was a requirement to use it every time he came home to ensure it stayed in working order.

We headed inside and I skipped through the foyer and into the main living room, which they used for lounging and gaming.

Trey looked up from his laptop and smiled. "Hello, Lily."

Hopping over the back of the couch, I landed on the cushion next to him. "Hello, Trey."

Frowning, he asked, "Are you having trouble sleeping?"

Sticking my lip out in a pout I asked, "Are you saying I look bad? This isn't the best way to start off our date, you know?"

He prodded just below my eyes. "You've got eyebags."

"I just stayed up too late," I admitted. Pulling the key from my bag I asked, "So, do I get to find out what this is for?"

Mason's eyes widened. "Trey," he growled.

Trey held up his hand and Mason went silent. "I should have known the ever-curious Lily would ask about the key first thing when she arrived. And here I thought you might be interested in me and the date I have planned."

"Why can't it be both?" I said and shrugged.

He stood and walked around the couch and waved at me. "Well, come on."

I followed him, my curiosity and excitement making me vibrate as I practically walked on his heels.

He led me down the hallway and to a metal door that I didn't remember from the one time I had been here before. "This leads to our secret room. So far, only Mason, Kayden, and I have been allowed in. We are now allowing you access as well."

The way he described it made it sound more like a man cave, a place they would go to escape life, than something truly cool. Was this a meaningless gesture, or was I about to see something cool that would truly portray their confidence in me? Also, he had said they were allowing me access, but Mason's growl hadn't seemed like he'd known about Trey giving me a key.

I looked at the key and looked at the door. The key had the same scrollwork design as the door. Walking up to it, I inserted the key and turned it, eyes widening as the lock clicked open.

Removing the key, I tried to open the door, but it was really heavy.

Trey chuckled. "Not as strong as you used to be, Princess?"

Giving him a quick glare, I grabbed the handle and pulled harder, now knowing it was a heavy door. It opened slowly and quietly. "Hinges are nicely oiled," I grunted as I finished opening it.

Soft red lights turned on, providing enough lighting for us to see as we walked down a staircase. Without waiting for confirmation of my permission to enter, I walked down the stairs, heart beating faster in anticipation as I headed for their secret room.

What could they keep down here that they didn't want others to know about? He'd said only they had a key, which meant not even his dad or the kings had a key?

As my foot hit the last steps, a bright light turned on, revealing a large circular room. In the center was a round stone table with a glass top and atop that were three laptops. In the very center was a large leather book that looked well worn.

Was that the demon journal Kayden had told me about?

On one wall was a map of the world with hundreds of red pins and a couple dozen purple pins.

There was also a small refrigerator, water cooler, sink, microwave, plastic side table with paper plates and snacks like chips and granola bars, and three couches with folded blankets and pillows.

"We call it our command center." Trey walked by me and sat in one of the chairs at the stone table.

"Kayden mentioned you had a book you were recording your knowledge on demons and depictions of them. Is that it?" I asked and pointed at the large leather book.

He nodded.

Looking at that book was my top priority, but I couldn't let him know that.

"That map, what do the different colored pins mean?" I turned away from the book to look at the map, so he wouldn't realize that was my goal.

"Red are singular portals. Purple are locations where multiple portals have opened," he answered.

I walked closer to inspect it, noticing the purple pins were almost always around main cities. "You think it has something to do with population density?" I asked and turned to face him.

"That's one of our current theories," he said with a nod.

Moving to the stone table, I sat in the chair beside his, then reached for the leather book, but looked at him for approval first.

He nodded. "I gave you that key so you could have access and, my hope was, that you would start helping us."

"You want me to help you how?" I asked as I greedily grabbed the book and pulled it towards me. I thumbed through the first few pages, but moved to the later part of the book where the drawings were. My eyes widened at the strange creatures they had drawn there; types I had never seen before.

"We've been going over our research for years with very little to show for it. No clue as to how or why the demons are coming more and more often. Perhaps, with a different set of eyes on it, you could see something we've been missing." He leaned forward. "The idea to go through the portal was brought up once, but we quickly nixed it, as we didn't want to risk being killed. However, Kayden mentioned your questions and suggestions and it definitely made me want to reconsider. How could we do it safely? How could we do some recon into the portal without us being injured?"

So, Kayden had told them, but it seemed he and Trey weren't exactly on the same page. "A camera?" I asked.

He shook his head. "We tried that, but a creature stepped out of the portal with the camera we had tossed through in his hand and snapped it in our faces so we couldn't get anything from it."

"I bet Kayden was livid when that happened," I said and chuckled as I imagined his reaction.

"Just a bit," Trey said with a soft laugh.

"Have you tried grabbing a smaller creature and tossing it back through with a rope around it, then pulling it back again to see if it gets injured?" I asked.

He frowned. "No."

"That would tell you with certainty if they get hurt going

back and forth at least before we test putting a person from our side through."

"That's a good idea. It is just dependent on us getting a portal with smaller creatures. It's about one out of every five."

"Have you tried talking to them? Are any of them capable of communication?"

"Not that we've encountered so far," he answered. "Though, to be fair, most of the time we attack them as soon as they come out, especially those big bull ones."

"So, there are quite a few things we need to try," I said with a nod as I resumed reading their notes. I pulled out my own notebook and compared theirs with what I'd found that I had thought was credible.

"What is that?" Trey asked, walking to stand behind me and looked over my shoulder.

"Notes I was making," I said and flipped past a few pages I didn't want him to read.

My phone rang in my bag. I pulled it out and scoffed at Luca's name on the screen. "He just doesn't know when to give up, does he?"

"Didn't Branson take him back his gifts?" Trey asked as he took his seat again.

I nodded. "He must have just done it, which is most likely why Luca's calling." I hit ignore and hoped he didn't leave a voicemail.

"So, any favorites on your dates so far?" Trey asked.

"A couple contenders so far," I whispered in reply, trying to focus on the section written about hellhounds, which were by the far the most commonly encountered demons.

"Any princes?" he asked.

"A couple," I replied again.

"A couple?" he asked, his tone confused.

Looking up, I asked, "Is this what your plan for the date was? Let me in here and let me read?"

Laughing, he shook his head and stood. "No, but I knew if I didn't let you read a bit of it, your curiosity would distract you from the rest of my date."

"Don't act like you know me," I teased and flipped my hair over my shoulder as I, reluctantly, turned away from the journal.

"You are welcome here any time that you wish to be. That's why I gave you a key." He followed me up the stairs. "There's a room for you as well, not for tonight, unless you want to stay tonight, but a room that is explicitly yours."

I stumbled on the step and started to fall, but he caught me and smirked as he looked at my face upside down.

"You have a what?"

Pushing me forward, he righted me so I could continue up the stairs to the main floor.

"Would you like to see it?"

Yes, but I felt like that should be a later event.

"What else did you have planned for today?" I asked instead. "Hopefully, food is involved." My stomach growled on cue. "I haven't been hunting since before my party." Eating regular food five times a day could keep me full, but even then, I still required a medium-sized animal once a week in my snake form. It was a weird condition that we had figured out when I started school. Eating more in human form still didn't satiate that hunger either.

"Would you like a quick hunt? Or regular food?"

"Regular food is fine. I'll hunt tomorrow."

"Can I join you tomorrow?" Mason asked from his spot on the couch in the living room, eyes focused on the screen as he played a video game.

"You want to hunt with me?" I asked.

He nodded.

"Sure," I said with a shrug, "I don't mind you coming."

"It could count as our second date," he said and glanced at us for a second before refocusing on his game.

"Well, now that my date has been interrupted by you setting up a date with another man, can we get back to ours?" Trey asked.

I rolled my eyes. "As if you care about me going on dates with Mas or Kay."

Trey stepped up right into my personal space and said, "I care very much about you going on dates with other men. Every moment you aren't near me is a moment I detest."

"That was smooth," I said and swallowed hard because … it hadn't been a lie. Or, perhaps my sensor was broken?

"Come, let's go get food," Trey said and spun away from me.

We walked out to the garage and got into a shiny red sportscar. His dad had bought it for him not realizing Trey hated red cars.

"Still haven't painted it?" I questioned as I snuggled into the soft seats.

Sighing, he said, "When I mentioned it, Dad got really sad, so I opted not to do it."

"We aren't taking Mason with us as a guard?" I asked.

"Obviously not."

"You sure that's okay?"

"If I didn't think it was, I would have had him follow us."

With no comeback to that, I sat silently.

We drove out of the garage and into the city.

"Where are we going?" Honestly, I would eat anything, so I wasn't worried, but I was curious.

"I have a reservation for us at a new place. The chef and owner are former friends of Dad's and I saved their son from a demon attack."

"How many people have you saved?" I asked.

He parked and said, "I don't keep track of how many people I save. That's not the kind of person I am, you should know that."

I shrugged. "We haven't talked in several years. I'm not certain what kind of man you are anymore."

"Hm," he said as he climbed out and walked around to open my door. Stepping out, he whispered in my ear, "Then I'll just have to prove what kind of man I am to you."

"That's what these dates are for, Trey. So, prove to me that you're the best option." With a wink, I walked by him and into the restaurant's front door.

The food was delicious, but we didn't get much time to talk since the owner and chef spent most of our time talking to Trey. My necklace had warmed a moment and then stopped and with no portal opening, I wondered if the other times had truly been coincidental or not.

We exited the restaurant, but the sound of screams had us running away from our car and to the park across the street.

The necklace warmed more and my feet moved on their own, towards something drawing me.

A large portal with two hellhounds and two bull-headed demons standing in front of it was open in the center of the park.

People surrounded it from fifty feet away, staring at the creatures who looked frozen if you didn't notice their chests moving as they breathed. They weren't even looking around, just ... standing.

"Ever seen this before?" I asked Trey as we joined the onlookers.

"No," he replied and dialed someone. "Portal on my location. Two bulls and two hounds. Something's off, hurry." He put his phone away and rolled up the sleeves of his shirt. "No rest for the wicked, eh?"

Walking forward slowly, I kept my hands at my sides, open so they could see I was unarmed. "Hello?" I called out.

The demon creatures all turned to look at me, eyes focused on me immediately.

People backed away quickly once the creatures moved.

"Lily!" Trey snapped. "Stay back."

"Let's do one of our tests," I whispered back. Smiling at the demon creatures I asked, "Can you speak? My name is Lily. Do you have names?"

The creatures moved forward, headed towards me, but didn't make any noise in any attempt to speak.

I backed up a step and held my hand up. "Stop."

They stopped.

"Uh ..." Trey whispered.

Well, they understood our speech at least.

"Go back through the portal," I ordered.

The two hellhounds turned and went back through the portal, but the bulls stayed.

"How is she commanding them?" an onlooker asked.

"Is this something the hybrids started? Did they create the demons?" another asked.

Why were people so quick to blame hybrids? The demons had been attacking far longer than my clan was created.

"What do you want?" I demanded. "Do you have a leader? Someone who is ordering you to do these attacks? Why are you here? Why do you keep coming here? Why are you attacking our people?"

The pull became stronger and I reached up, clutching the necklace as it throbbed against my chest almost painfully.

What was through that portal? What would I find on the other side?

The urge to run through was so strong I had to close my eyes and bite the side of my mouth until I drew blood to stop.

The bulls moved forward and reached for me, but I ducked out of the way before they could touch me and Trey kicked the closest one in the chest, making him stumble back a few steps.

The two hellhounds walked out of the portal again, snarling this time.

"Well, two questions answered," I muttered to Trey as he and I started ducking and dodging the bulls who were trying to grab me. "They aren't interested in communicating, or can't, but can understand our language. And they can come and go through the portals without getting injured."

I ran around the portal, trying to put distance between me and the creatures, but the bulls followed me. It seemed like they were completely unconcerned with Trey and only cared about grabbing me. Their beefy hands reached out anytime they got close, trying to grasp my arm or my hair, but they weren't attacking me so far.

The hellhounds leapt at Trey, forcing him to take a warrior shift and knock them away with his tail.

"Get farther back," Trey ordered everyone, including me.

One of the hellhounds jumped towards me and I kicked it in the face, its bone crunching and jaw hanging off its face at a weird angle. Still, it came after me, but not growling like it did when it faced Trey.

Trey breathed fire onto the injured hellhound and it disintegrated.

Distracted by the hellhound and trying to get away from one of the bulls, the second one grabbed my arm and started dragging me towards the portal.

I gasped, stuck my heels in the ground, grabbed his arm, and snapped the bone in half.

He bellowed in pain, released me, and tried to backhand me.

Ducking under his backhand, I rolled away from him and towards Trey.

Mason flew down towards us in raven form, landing on the bull-man with the broken arm's head, and pecked at his eyes, blinding him.

The bull-man bellowed and started to fall backwards through the portal, with Mason on his head.

"Mason!" I screamed in fear.

He flew off of the bull-man's head and circled around before shifting and landing on human feet behind me. "Are you injured?"

"No," I whispered.

Trey killed the last hellhound and all the bodies disintegrated into black smoke.

Mason grabbed my shoulder and jerked me back. "Lily!"

I blinked, shocked to find I was less than two feet from the portal, my hand wrapped around the necklace.

Dropping my hand, the pull lessened, but not fully.

After another thirty seconds, the portal closed and disappeared.

Relief coursed through me and I started to fall, but Trey caught me and picked me up with an arm beneath my legs and one behind my back. "I've got you, Princess."

CHAPTER

THIRTEEN

"I warned you that there was something off about her interest in the demons!" Kayden yelled.

"There's nothing off about her interest. We're just as interested as her, she's just more willing to act than us," Trey argued.

"You put her at risk," Kayden growled.

"I protected her," Trey growled back.

"Why are they after her? Does it have to do with the pull we feel, too?" Mason asked softly.

Pull they felt? What was he talking about?

Someone's phone rang.

"It's Caleb," Kayden muttered.

"Answer it, idiot. He likely saw news footage of the attack," Trey said.

My phone pinged with a text and all three growled.

"Why is that elf prince messaging her?" Mason grumbled.

I was laying down, most likely on a couch, on my back.

Rolling onto my side, I sat up and rubbed my eyes. "What's going on? What happened?"

All three sat on the couch opposite me.

"Here," Kayden said and held out his phone.

"Hello?" I answered as I took it.

"Why did you approach the portal?" Caleb asked.

"Uh, about that. I was trying to see if the creatures might be non-hostile and communicate with us. No one has really tried to communicate with them before. I figured it was worth a try."

He sighed so loud I had to pull the phone away from my ear.

"I'm uninjured," I said, "so no need to worry. I'll call you later. Love you, bye." I hung up and tossed the phone back to Kayden. "Where's my phone? Did anyone else try to call?"

"No one important," Mason muttered, but held out my phone.

"So, what's next on our date?" I asked Trey with a wide smile.

"Swimming," he answered.

Mason and Kayden gaped at him. I was also surprised by his agreeing to change the topic so quickly and not ask me the million questions likely on their minds.

"I don't have a bathing suit. You didn't warn me in advance."

He smiled. "Shifted swimming."

My eyes widened and I gasped. "Really?"

"You're just going to continue your date and not ask the questions we need to ask?" Kayden demanded. "Not try to figure out what's going on?"

Trey grabbed a duffel bag and slung it over his shoulder. "You can ask her whatever questions you want on your date. I'm not wasting my time."

I blew Kayden a kiss and skipped after Trey, humming loudly because Kayden hated humming.

He gave me my wanted growl, making me smile wider.

"You've always angered him on purpose and I've always enjoyed it," Trey said as we walked out the back door and down a concrete path lined with small solar lights that gave off just enough light to keep you on the path.

"How have you been?" I asked Trey. "Is traveling and hunting demons all it's cracked up to be?"

"There have been rough days," he said with a nod. "Most of the time, it's just been one fight after another, simplistic and fun. There were a few times when one of them got injured enough to worry me, but they pulled through."

"I heard your mom set you up on blind dates."

He stopped so abruptly I almost ran into him. Turning around, he looked down at me with a scowl. "Who told you?"

"Does it matter?"

He growled and resumed walking until we got to a large lake. The manmade lake was constantly stocked with fish and was always warm thanks to a spell by the former Mage King, Johann, Grandpa Nico's father. The lake bordered the Den and Trey's property.

"Yes, I went on a few dates that my mother set up," he finally answered as we took our shoes off at the lake's shore.

One great thing about our shifting abilities was that it somehow interacted with our clothing, too. So, I could shift and then when I returned to human form, I would have my clothes back on. Shifting into a warrior form so I could have scales all over my body, but still be able to talk, I jumped into the water and sighed in relief. "Seems like none of them worked out? Why not?"

He swam out to me in warrior form with scales covering his body as well. His bluish scales reflected the moonlight, casting beautiful colors atop the water around him.

"Because they weren't you," he answered.

The truthful, sudden statement made me stop treading water for a moment, my head going beneath the surface before I spluttered and kicked my legs to get above the water and breath again. My heart pounded in my chest and my mouth hung open.

Trey swam in a circle around me. "I missed you more than I thought it was possible to miss someone who is alive. We would walk through a city and I could swear I smelled you, but when I turned ... you weren't there. I wanted to call you so many times, but you blocked us. I considered changing my number so I could call you, but I also wanted to respect your wishes. I tried to figure out why you blocked us, what could have possibly happened to upset you so much. There were several times I was about to hop on a jet to fly to you, but the investigator I hired claimed you were dating Luca."

I scoffed.

"Yes, I should have hired a better investigator, obviously. It was when I heard you were dating him that I agreed to the dates my mother set up." He smiled, showing off dragon's teeth in his mostly human face. "I figured if you were doing it then so should I. I had hoped it would ease some of my pain, but all it did was intensify it. You are like a fire and I'm a moth." He swam closer to me until he was treading water just in front of me. "I would gladly burn if it meant you accepted me as a mate."

Toads on a stool. He was serious. One hundred percent honest.

"And what if I stepped through a demon portal?" I asked.

He put an arm around me beneath the water and I wrapped my legs around his waist, letting him keep us both afloat. Knowing he would keep me safe, even if it meant drowning himself. "I would follow you through the deepest, darkest depths of the demon world. Life is only bearable with you in it. I know you're courting the others and I know you deserve the best, and I may not be it, but I can promise you that I will love you with my entire being this lifetime and the next, and you are the only woman for me. You've been the only woman for me since we made that promise as kids."

Shifting into my fully human form, not caring that my dress was now wet, I leaned forward and pressed my lips to his. His scales disappeared as he hugged me tighter and kissed me back. Swimming towards the shallower area so he could stand, he slid his hands up my back beneath my dress, stroking my skin as we kissed. Heat built within me, my core throbbed with need, and I had to resist grinding against him. He must have sensed it because he reached between us, pushed my underwear to the side, and slid a finger into me.

We both groaned. I rested my forehead against his shoulder as he pumped his finger in and out of me, stroking the fire within me. My stomach coiled tighter and tighter.

"I want to see your face, Princess, when I make you

come," he said and wiggled his shoulder beneath my forehead.

Leaning back, I stared into his bright eyes, mesmerized by the bit of darkness in his aura that was swirling maniacally now.

He withdrew his finger and before I could complain, he slid two fingers back into me, pumping faster and harder.

My fingers dug into his shoulder as I panted.

Leaning forward, he kissed, licked, and nipped at my throat, making an almost purring sound. "Come for me, beautiful. I promise this is just the first of many pleasurable encounters." Moving his other hand where it had been pressed against my back, he slid it around to cup my breast, squeezing and massaging.

"Yes," I gasped and threw my head back, grinding against his hand as he continued to finger me.

When he moved his thumb up to rub at my clit while he fingered me, my grinding increased. Had this been Liam or one of the men I hadn't known, I might have been embarrassed, but not with Trey. This was a long time coming ... pun totally intended.

He bit down on my neck, though not hard enough to break skin or mark me, it was just the push I needed to send me over the edge.

I screamed his name as I came, but he didn't stop pumping his fingers in and out of me until I had fully stopped with the aftershocks. I pressed my lips to his and he kissed me back.

He pulled back first and said, "I've dreamt of kissing you again a million times, Lily, of doing a lot of things to you, what happened just now included, but none of those fantasies involved us being in a lake."

Laughing, I pushed away from him and shifted into my full snake form, swimming out into the depths with a joyous feeling that had grown since Kayden had kissed me, then Mason, and now Trey.

Was this ... love? Or was it just the lust talking?

As I looked back at Trey, I saw the darkness in his aura had expanded more than I had noticed before. It was similar to Mason's, but not as strong yet.

Was it me? Was I ... infecting them?

Was the spell spreading to them somehow?

A large, red dragon swooped out of the sky, talons extended, and tried to grab me out of the lake.

I dove down beneath the water, avoiding their grab, and swam back towards Trey, keeping beneath the water.

Surfacing, I heard him shouting at someone and heard a feminine voice responding.

Turning, I sighed at the sight of Norma, one of my nemeses from high school. She had always hated that the trio spent most of their time around me and because of that, her and her posse had tried to bully me.

Things hadn't gone the way she had expected since I wasn't one to be bullied.

"Fucking Norma," I whispered before smiling and waving. "Oh, hey! Norma! It's been so long since I saw you. What's new?"

She was in her human form, standing on the shore with an innocent expression on her face. At my voice, her face hardened and she turned to give me the most ridiculous attempt at a smile I had ever seen.

"Oh, Lily. It *is* you. I was just telling Prince Trey that I thought you were a real snake and was trying to protect the children by grabbing you."

"Really?" I asked and frowned. "Since when do you care about children?"

She opened her mouth and closed it, her brows furrowed.

"Get out of here, Norma," Trey ordered her.

"This lake is for all *dragons* to use," she countered and flipped her hair over her shoulder.

"And yet all I see is a pretentious mouse," I said with a wide smile.

She growled and walked towards me. "Say that again, *snake*."

"Do you need hearing aids on top of an attitude adjustment?" I asked pleasantly, then lowering my voice said, "All I see is a pretentious mouse. If you think you've got the guts, fight me, bitch. We know how that ended for you last time." With her head in a trash bin.

"You've always thought you were tough with the trio at your back, but alone, you're nothing!" she spat.

"Trey, I order you to stand back and allow me to fight this asshole," I snarled.

Trey sighed, sat down cross-legged, and waved his hand towards us like a bored king waving at a jester to continue. "Proceed."

Cracking my knuckles, I smiled viciously as I approached her. "This is going to feel *so* good." Loosening my hold on the anger, I let it out to swirl around me, breathing a sigh of relief as it filled me. My hair glowed brighter and brighter, the closer I got to her and the more I let the anger out.

Dark electricity whipped around me, sizzling and hissing. My face shifted, turning partially snake-like, including scales, fangs, and a forked tongue.

She shifted into her full dragon form and spewed flames at me.

Jumping and rolling to the right, I avoided the flames. I flung my hand towards her, which sent electric tentacles out to slash her across the face and across the wings.

She screeched in pain and stumbled backwards.

With me, she would find no quarter. No leniency.

I leapt onto her back and tore into her, breaking the bone and tearing one of the wings from her back.

She screamed and I realized it was a human scream as she had shifted back to human form. She lay bleeding and crying, but it wasn't enough.

The torment she had inflicted upon me and, more importantly, others, was not so simply ignored. The anger within me wanted more blood. More pain.

Trey stood before me, the darkness in his aura swirling higher. "Lily?" he whispered.

"Blood," I whispered back. "There's not ... enough."

"You're a monster," Norma cried.

"You tormented me. Forced your posse to come after me. You tried to pluck me from the lake while I was reuniting with a friend and on a courting date. You are a monster. You are a piece of trash that should be burned away from this planet!"

She cowered and backed away from us, crawling on her hands.

Mason ran out to us with Kayden right on his heels.

"Lily?" Mason asked. "Can you shove it down?"

Looking at the three of them, I realized they all had the darkness.

Maybe ... maybe Norma was right about me being a monster.

"The darkness ... it's infected you three."

"What are you talking about?" Trey asked.

I waved my hand at them. "You've got darkness in your aura. Darkness that you've gained. Darkness like mine. Did ... did I infect you?"

Mason's eyes widened. "You can see auras, too?"

"'Too?'" I asked back.

"She tore my wing from my back!" Norma screeched at Trey behind us.

I spun, but Mason and Kayden each grabbed an arm to keep me from approaching her. "I know what you did to Estelle!"

Norma flinched. "Wh-What?"

Estelle was a chicken shifter, an extremely rare form that had earned her a lot of ridicule. "You plucked her feathers, every single one of them. Then, you told every guy who showed interest in her that she had a disease and that's why her feathers had fallen out."

"I-I didn't."

"She almost killed herself, Norma!" I screamed. "I stopped her, barely. That is not an easily forgiven incident. You are a piece of trash! Trash should burn!"

I tried to rush her again, but Trey grabbed me by the face and kissed me, distracting me from my fury.

"Take Lily to the house," Trey whispered. "I'll deal with ... her."

Kayden led the way while Mason walked behind me, forcing me to walk down the path back towards their house.

Collapsing on the couch, a warm blanket was set on me and I closed my eyes, feeling the pull of sleep.

"We're here, Lil'. Go to sleep," Kayden whispered.

"Blood," I whispered.

"Tomorrow," Mason promised. "We will hunt tomorrow."

I nodded and pulled the blanket up to my chin. "Tomorrow."

CHAPTER
FOURTEEN

I awoke on the couch, the trio sleeping nearby, and hurried down to the command center to read more about demons.

There was no information that helped with the draw I felt or the incident last night.

Honestly, I knew the incident yesterday had nothing to do with the demons or the necklace though.

I tried to remove the necklace, but when I reached to unclasp it, my fingers shook so hard I couldn't even grasp it, and I ultimately couldn't force myself to do it.

"I figured I would find you here," Trey said as he walked down the stairs and sat at the table next to me. He wore a pair of black sweatpants and a matching black t-shirt and his normally perfectly styled hair was messy.

"I'm sorry," I whispered, "about last night. I ..."

"You don't need to apologize. We knew she was an awful person before we knew about what she'd done to Estelle or her picking on you. It solidified the assumptions we already had about her, though."

"With this darkness ... I don't think I'm suited to be a prince's mate," I whispered.

He scooted his chair closer to mine, kissed my cheek, and said, "Darlin', you are perfectly suited to be a prince's or a king's mate. You stand up for the weak, for those who can't stand up for themselves. That's precisely what the clans need."

"Can we schedule another date?" I asked softly. "I feel like I messed up your plans significantly."

"I would love to schedule another date," he said with a smile and brushed some hair that had fallen into my face behind my ear.

"Lily?" Mason called as he ran down the stairs. He exhaled and sagged against the wall of the stairway. "You are here, phew."

"Did you think I ran away?" I asked.

He shrugged. "The thought had crossed my mind."

"Today's hunting day, remember?" I said with a smile.

He returned my smile, but it quickly disappeared when Kayden said, "And our date."

Right! The concert!

"I'll pick you up at six, okay?" Kayden said.

"Okay," I agreed. Changing the subject, I said, "I had an idea in my dreams. What if we use a phone, on a live video-call, attach it to a rope, and slide it through the portal? Then, if it gets destroyed, hopefully, we'll get a little video first. And maybe, if we're lucky, there won't be bull-men and we can pull the phone back having learned a bit more about their side of the portal."

"I like it," Trey said with a nod.

"Sounds good to me," Mason agreed.

"Only if she's not the one to put the item through," Kayden said and folded his arms across his chest.

"I'm hurt and annoyed by that statement," I admitted aloud.

"We can buy a burner phone while Mas and Lily are hunting," Trey said to Kayden. "And figure out a rope system that will work."

"I think we should ensure she's not nearby at all," Kayden said.

"Why *did* you walk towards the portal?" Mason asked.

"I felt it was safe to approach," I said, since that was true and didn't reveal more than that to them.

"You felt a portal to the demon world was *safe* to approach?" Kayden asked and ran a hand down his face. "You're going to be the death of me. I just know it."

I flinched, feeling like he had physically slapped me. "Mason, let's go. Seems I've overstayed my welcome." Turning to Trey, I smiled, and said, "I had a wonderful time on our date. I'll be in touch to schedule our second date."

Trey stood, grabbed my waist, and pulled me against him, kissing me deeply. His tongue stroked mine and I put my arms around his neck as I returned the kiss. Pulling back, panting, he said, "Don't put our date off for too long, okay?"

Finding it difficult to speak, I nodded, and quickly went up the stairs, unless I gave into the temptation to find out what they would do if I instigated something with all three present at the same time.

The idea had me wet all over again, but I ignored the

desire, grabbed my bag from the couch, and climbed into Mason's car so he could drive me home.

We drove in silence, once again, but it was nice not to answer questions or feel the need to apologize again.

I lucked out with no one downstairs, so I tossed my bag inside the door, shut it, and ran towards Mason who was halfway down the road towards the area of the forest we preferred to hunt in.

"Ready?" he asked.

I nodded and waved. "Lead the way, eagle eyes."

He glared at me, spun around, and said, "Ravens have great eyesight, too."

Laughing silently, I clasped my hands behind my back and skipped beside him. "So, have you done anymore reconnaissance missions?" Kieran was a hawk shifter and he had often been used for spying, but when he settled down with Sheila, he had started training Mason to be his replacement. Ravens were even more common than hawks, so it made him even better as a spy since people would pay no mind to a raven flying around.

"I've done a few," he said as he continued to lead the way deep into the forest that we owned. With so many predators in one area, the prey tended to stay farther away, so we had to head pretty deep into the forest to hunt.

"Any fun ones?" I asked.

"Most recon missions are boring," he admitted. "Listening to people discussing secrets then reporting that back to one of the kings. They don't let me fight them or try to capture them, so it's not much fun."

Of course, Mason would hate a mission where he didn't get to punch someone.

He paused next to a tree with narrowed eyes.

I froze, assuming he could see an animal we could hunt.

Glancing over his shoulder at me, he asked, "Did you have sex with Trey last night?"

My eyes widened at the sudden question, but I answered immediately, "No."

He nodded. "Okay."

We resumed walking and I noticed the muscles in his back had relaxed a bit. Clearly, he'd been concerned I had slept with Trey. But why? Because he wanted to be first, or was it something else?

He stopped again and immediately shifted.

I shifted as well, assuming he'd seen something for us to hunt. My assumption was right when I saw a large jackrabbit walk into my view. It was the perfect size to allow me to eat, satiate my hunting desire, but finish digesting it before the evening and my date with Kayden. Normally, if I had no plans, I would eat something like a boar or a deer, but I rarely had time without plans.

Flattening myself as much as possible, I slithered closer until I was within striking distance, then struck. The jackrabbit squealed and tried to run away, but my jaw was firmly locked around the back of its neck and I encircled its body with one of my coils, wrapping tighter and tighter until it couldn't move.

Once it was dead, I released it and moved back to let Mason eat first. As a constrictor, I would swallow the jackrabbit whole, so I needed to give him time to eat before that.

Once he had his fill, he made an odd honk sound, then flew up into a tree nearby.

Beginning the slow and tedious process of swallowing the rabbit, I let my mind drift into peaceful oblivion, focused on the sole task at hand.

Once swallowed, I closed my eyes and lay still to digest it, knowing Mason would keep me safe.

Occasionally, I heard him fly from his post to attack something, to eat more, but since he didn't make any noises to alert me, I continued to nap.

After finally digesting enough to shift, I stood and dusted myself off. "Thank you, for coming with me."

He flew over my head in a circle and croaked, "Good hunt."

Sometimes it was eerie how he could speak in an almost human voice like that. It had nothing to do with him being a shifter and was one hundred percent him being a raven. They could mimic sounds really well.

"Yes, it was a good hunt. Now, I need to head back to the house to shower and change."

Flying overhead, he followed me to the house. Once at the house, he shifted and walked inside.

"Uh, what are you doing?" I asked, following him inside and up the stairs.

Once again, no one was home. What were they all working on away from home? Sure, they had several businesses, but they mostly ran themselves. It must not have been urgent or they would have told me. Right? Or were they keeping me out of it since I had asked for a hiatus between college ending and me taking my place as princess?

"I need a shower, too. So, let's kill two birds with one stone," he answered and stripped his shirt off with one swift pull.

Why did that shirt removal make me horny? It was smooth, but still ...

"You want to shower with me?" I asked.

He looked over his shoulder at me. "That was the plan." Without waiting for my response, he opened my bedroom door, tossed his shirt on my bed, removed his sweatpants, tossed them on the bed, and headed to the bathroom.

I stared at his naked, muscular ass as he walked away, mesmerized. He had one of the nicest asses I had seen on a man. I wanted to take a bite out of it.

After locking my bedroom door, I stripped out of my dress and undergarments, and followed him, deciding it was now or never to do the things I had always wanted to do. Plus, wouldn't this help me figure out if they were the ones meant to be my mates? Wasn't this part of courting?

The shower was running and steam was already rising up towards the ceiling as I entered.

Freezing at the door to the shower, I stared at his frosted outline. What if he didn't like me? What if he found fault with the parts of my body that I already found faults with?

Mentally cussing at myself and the ridiculousness of those thoughts, I opened the shower door and stepped inside.

My eyes immediately dropped to his delicious ass now covered in water and there for grabbing.

"My eyes are up here," he said, surprising me out of my thoughts so much I jumped.

When I raised my eyes, I found him smiling one of his rare, true smiles. "Can you blame me? You've got an amazing ass."

His smile widened and he stepped to the side so I could get under the water. "Thank you for the compliment." His eyes slowly roved down my body and back up to my face. "You are perfection personified."

Stepping into the warm water, I put my hands on his chest and asked, "Why did you ask if I slept with Trey? Aren't you all a packaged deal?"

"In a sense," he said, "but I had hoped that I might be your first."

"Is this a pissing contest between you three?" I asked with a scowl and stepped back.

He shook his head. "No, nothing like that. I'm sorry. I shouldn't have asked."

"Are you worried I care about them more than you?"

Turning his head away, he nodded.

Sliding my hand along his cheek farthest from me, I pulled him back to face me. "Mason, you are not less than Trey or Kayden. I have *never, ever* thought of you as less than them. I swear it on my mother."

His eyes widened at my sincerity.

My eyes dropped to his collarbone where he had a tattoo that wrapped from his collarbone around his chest and down to his stomach. The tattoo was of a suspiciously familiar snake. "Is ... Is that me?"

He glanced down at his chest and nodded.

My fingers traced the snake and he shuddered beneath my touch. "You got me tattooed on you?"

"Over my heart, where you will always be," he said with a nod.

"What if ... what if I choose a different mate?" I asked, not daring to look up at him.

"It doesn't change that you will always be the one who has my heart and soul."

Sucking in a shuddering breath, I looked up at him, "I don't know if I can live up to or be what you would want or need me to be. I'm always trying to fit in a role that I don't think I'm fit to be in. I shouldn't be a princess with this darkness, this desire for blood and destruction that's getting stronger as I get older. Should I even have mates, let alone strong alphas like you when you should be furthering our species with another strong hybrid or someone from one of the other clans?"

His brows furrowed. "You are more than your title. You are one of the most amazing women I have ever encountered. I have traveled all over this world, met many women, and you are by far the only one who has ever captured my attention."

"That's only because you knew me growing up. Because you were basically groomed to want to have me as a mate."

This negative talk wasn't something I normally allowed or accepted within myself. Why was it happening more and more often?

Mason gripped me by my neck, tilted my head up, and glared down into my eyes. "You are the greatest woman in existence. It's absolutely ridiculous of me to even breathe the same air as you, let alone be able to view your perfect naked body or touch it. Even though you won't be queen, you *are* a queen. You always have been in my eyes. I would follow you to the ends of the universe so long as it meant spending more time in your presence."

"I—"

He pressed his lips to mine, his arm wrapped around my lower back, and he pushed me back against the wall of the shower. His erection pulsed between us and I wanted him in me more than I wanted anything ever.

"Please," I begged him. "I want you, Mason. Please."

"This had not been my plan," he said as he kissed his way down my throat and between my breasts. "I'd wanted to fool around, but not—"

"Mason, I don't care what your plan was," I snapped and reached down between us to grip his erection.

He moaned and thrust into my hand. His hand slid down until he slipped two fingers inside of me, feeling how wet I was. Removing his fingers, he grabbed my hips, lifted me up, and impaled me on his cock, thrusting into me as he pushed me against the wall of the shower.

"Yes!" I screamed, put my arms around his neck, and rode him as he thrust into me.

He licked and sucked at my neck, moving down to suck my nipple into his mouth.

I gasped and arched back, giving him easier access and enjoying the way it felt.

His tongue lapped at my nipple as I rode him and came, screaming his name.

He found his relief soon after, grunting and biting gently

into my shoulder, but thankfully not enough to mark me ... yet.

"What did you mean about feeling a pull to me?" I asked as he washed me with a soapy loofa. Mason had insisted on washing me to erase his scent, not because he was embarrassed or didn't want others to know, but because he thought it might upset Kayden, who was supposed to pick me up in less than two hours.

"You know how it feels to be around Leona and Jolie, that addictive joy? It's sort of like that, but there's also a literal pull, like you're a magnet and we're metal drawn to you. I could close my eyes and as you moved around a room, I would know exactly where you are."

"How long have you felt that?" I asked, my throat feeling tighter.

He continued washing me gently, so careful and tender, so unlike Mason was in everyday life, especially with others. He had always been kind to me, more so than with others, but this was another level than what I'd experienced. "I've felt this way since we were teenagers I believe, but it could have started before that."

I needed to talk to Great Aunt Leona. I needed to find out if there was a way to stop this from happening. Even if that meant they were no longer interested in me.

FIFTEEN

I'd promised to message Mason with a day for our second date tomorrow after I had a chance to look over my calendar. I needed to schedule second dates with Liam, Trey, and Mason.

Remembering Liam had messaged me after the demon incident, I called him back.

"Are you okay?" he asked as soon as he picked up. "I saw the video and saw you pass out at the end."

"Yes, I'm okay. I appreciate your concern," I replied.

He exhaled. "That's good to hear. I was worried. I know you must be busy so I won't take up more of your time, but I am looking forward to our next date."

"I'll send you a couple available dates soon. Things have been crazy so I apologize."

"No need to apologize. I will look forward to your text. Have a great evening."

"You as well, Liam."

We hung up and I stared at the phone. He was a really

nice guy. I needed to do something that allowed us to talk and interact more on our next date to get to know him better. The one major red flag for me was his goal of living a super simplistic life on the other side of the ocean. That was not in line with my goal of helping my clan at all.

"He's here!" Mom yelled from downstairs.

I texted Great Aunt Leona to ask if I could talk to her tomorrow, grabbed the tickets, slipped my phone in my pocket, and jogged down the stairs.

"How do I look?" I asked Mom.

She inspected my tight jeans, crop top, and choker necklace in addition to the necklace the trio had given me, since I still couldn't remove it, and darker than usual makeup and nodded. I'd also put my hair up in a ponytail to keep it out of my face since I was absolutely going to end up dancing to the songs. "Definitely concert appropriate. It's going to get hot in that venue with all those people."

"Hello," Kayden greeted me with a smile as I opened the front door. He looked at my outfit and smiled as he said, "You look great."

He wore a pair of jeans that might as well have been painted on and a t-shirt that was the same, with an image of a snake curled around a music note.

"Where did you find that shirt?" I asked, mouth dropped open.

"I had it custom printed. Do you like it?" He smiled, grabbed a corner of the shirt, and tugged it up to make it move.

"How do I get one?" I asked.

He leaned forward until his lips were right by my ear and said, "You ask me really, really nicely."

In a sickly-sweet tone, I whispered, "Give me a fucking shirt."

He threw his head back as he laughed and took a step back, putting space between us.

"You leaving on your date already?" Mom asked.

"Yes, bye. Love you."

"Don't let him mark you!" Dad yelled from the dining room.

Kayden made a strange growling grunt, spun away, and marched down the driveway.

"Aw, you upset the pup," Triston said in a taunting tone.

"Could you act like my fathers for like four seconds?" I hissed.

"No!" Caleb, Triston, Riddick, and Branson all yelled back at me.

Sighing loudly, I shut the door and followed Kayden. "I apologize for my ridiculous fathers. Having more than one definitely causes issues. Sorry!"

We got into a black SUV totally decked out with bullet-proof and magic-proof windows that were also tinted so you could not see the person inside. The SUV also had reinforced armor and even a mini-turret that popped up on the roof.

"Really, how did you get these tickets?" I asked as I buckled my seatbelt. "I tried and couldn't get them before they sold out."

"I saved the drummer's wife from a demon," Kayden answered.

My eyes widened as I gasped. "Whoa."

"Yeah, it was a really crazy day," he admitted.

We went silent for a bit before I finally broke it.

"Are you sure you want to do this?" I asked. "Are you sure you want to court me? What if you find a better woman ... somewhere else?"

He scoffed. "I've been all around the world. There are no better women. Trust me."

"Or, like I said to Mason, you're just groomed into thinking that."

The car veered off the road to the shoulder, slid to a stop, and he spun to look at me. "Where is this coming from?"

Taking a deep breath, I spit it all out as quick as I could. "I think the spell that was used on me, the darkness from it, infected you three, and I'm concerned that it altered you three into being focused on me and that's why you feel drawn to me."

"Or," he said and leaned across the center console to stare right in my eyes, "we've been obsessed with you because you were our best friend and we enjoy spending time with you."

"Mason said you guys feel a pull to me, that it's similar to what people feel around sirens. The spell used on me was a mixture of siren and mage magic. It could be—"

He shook his head. "It doesn't matter what it could be. What matters is we care about you and want to be with you. What matters is how you feel about us. I think this negative self-talk is from the spell as well. It alters your emotions and self-deprecation is not an emotion you genuinely have."

He could be right. It was another thing I would have to talk to Leona about.

Reaching forward, he stroked his fingers along my cheek and continued back until he cupped the back of my neck.

My body warmed and I arched my upper body towards him.

"Listen to me, Liliana Rubyserpent. You are beautiful, smart, kind, cunning, and a goddess who deserves to be worshipped. No matter what happens, no matter what path you go down, I will always have your back. I may bitch about it and growl a lot, but I will never forsake you. Even when you blocked us, I demanded Trey send an investigator to at least confirm you were doing well, I asked Dad about you constantly and made him promise not to tell you. We never gave up on our goal of coming back to take you as our mate. Did we bungle it a bit? Yes, obviously. Are there things I would change? One hundred percent. However, my goal has always been to be whatever you want me to be. You want a guard? I'll do it. You want a friend to cry on? I'll be here with tissues ready. I know I was terrible at showing it. I know I fucked things up by not explaining my feelings sooner. I know I hurt you. I know you're still hurt by it, even though you haven't said anything. I'm a rash idiot at the best of times, but I have been working every single day on becoming the best male I can be to ensure I am here to help you in any way that you might need. Not for fame, not for bettering our clan, but for you. So, stop worrying about what may or may not have caused my loyalty. Just embrace and accept it, and do what is best for you and know I will follow. Okay?"

Tears silently slipped down my face at his speech and a warmth grew in my chest that I hadn't realized was cold. Leaning forward, I pressed my lips lightly against his before I pulled back and said, "I will do *my* best to earn your continued loyalty."

He used his thumbs to wipe the tears from my face and said, "Just keep being you, Lily." He pressed a kiss to my forehead and my eyes fluttered closed. "Just keep being you."

WE MADE it to the concert without any other discussion and I felt lighter than I had in years.

After parking in the VIP section, signing about a dozen people's tickets, and taking selfies with at least two dozen groups, we finally made it to our seats. In the front row!

"Always so popular," he teased as we sat.

Ignoring his taunt, I bounced on my seat. "I've never been in the front row of one of their concerts before! I'm excited!"

"Why haven't you? You're a princess, pretty sure their record label would dive at a chance to say you were attending."

"I don't like to use my status as princess to get me things," I explained. "I logged onto their sales page just like everyone else each time I tried to get tickets. Most of the time my luck was bad and I didn't get a single ticket or the ones I did get were pretty far back."

"Well, I hope this is a performance you'll always remember," he said.

Turning, I smiled at him. "It's our first concert together,

so I'll definitely remember it. Plus, they can't have a bad performance. They're amazing."

A man in a pair of black slacks and a white button-up shirt hurried over to us and bowed. "Your Highness, we are delighted that you are attending the concert. Due to your status, we understand it would be difficult to get drinks and snacks, so I will be here to assist with that and merchandise as well. Please let me know what you'd like and I will obtain it for you. My name is Bart. The band members have also requested the two of you have a meet and greet with them backstage."

"Oh, you don't have to do all of that!" I said with wide eyes.

"It will be difficult to make it through the snack lines," Kayden said. "And I'm not going to leave you alone to go without you."

Gnawing on my lip, I finally conceded when I realized he was right. "Okay." I gave him my order and Kayden gave him his. Once he had the orders, he hurried off to get the items.

"Don't pout because you're being given special treatment," Kayden said while laughing.

"You know I hate special treatment for being princess."

"You only hate it because you feel like you don't deserve it because you're adopted, which is absolutely ridiculous. You've done just as much, if not more, for the hybrid clan than Tony has."

"I haven't done enough," I said softly, hating that he knew me so well.

"When would it be enough?" he asked. "You and Ember worked together to open that orphanage. I know you go visit them multiple times a year and bring all of the orphans holiday gifts and forced news outlets to take down articles mentioning it because you didn't want people to think it was a publicity stunt."

"How did you—"

"Like I said, I've been asking about you."

"More like stalking me," I whispered in mock horror.

He laughed and shrugged. "In a sense, I guess, I have been."

"Speaking of stalking, what happened with the guy who attacked me at my party?" I hadn't asked about it yet.

"I caught him and barely stopped Mas from killing him, then we took him for questioning. From what we can tell, he was acting alone and had a grudge against Ember from back when she lived in the woods and he lived in the city nearby. He figured your death would hurt her."

It would have. Mom might have destroyed the city in her fury. It was one of the reasons we had all started meditating. We were more powerful than a lot of full-blooded people and some of us, like Mom with her telekinesis powers, could very easily destroy a city if she were upset enough.

"Well, that's reassuring to hear," I admitted. "It should mean that I don't have to be on my toes, at least more than usual."

He draped an arm on the back of my chair, winked, and said, "Plus, I'm here."

Bart returned with a second person, carrying our ordered drinks, snacks, and a concert t-shirt for me.

"Thank you, I really appreciate you getting these things for me," I said to the two employees.

"Of course, Your Highness. Is there anything else that you need right now?"

I shook my head. "No, thank you. This should tide us over for the concert."

"Please don't hesitate to raise your hand should you need something," he said, bowed, and they both walked away.

"Did you know this is my first ever concert t-shirt?" I asked Kayden.

"What? How?"

"Like you said, it's difficult to get through the lines and the last time I did go to a concert, I hadn't wanted to ask your dad to leave me to get a shirt."

"Man, I'm popping several of your cherries tonight, aren't I?" he teased with a wink.

I rolled my eyes and turned to face the stage while taking a drink of the beer I had ordered. The crew were finishing the setup, which meant the band would come out soon.

One of the crew, a man in his early twenties with wild hair, rushed towards us, squatting down so he could speak. "Good evening, the band has requested Kayden come see them as well as Your Highness. Can you please go to the stairs there?" He pointed to our left where a security guard stood.

"What about our stuff?" I asked Kayden. "Should we grab it?"

Bart rushed over. "I shall stay in your seat, Your Highness, to ensure no one touches your items."

"Thank you!" I chirped with a smile, stood, and headed towards the stairs.

Kayden followed on my heels, but when he got up to the security guard, he bumped fists with him.

I arched a brow and he said, "He's one of Dad's friends from the werewolf pack."

The guard bowed his head to me and moved to the side so we could climb up the stairs.

Kayden put his hand on my lower back as we followed the crewmember into the back, behind the stage, and to a room where the bandmembers were relaxing on couches.

Grabbing Kayden's shirt, I whispered, "It's really them!" The members of my favorite band, *The Avery's*, looked just like they always did, handsome and talented. They had been a band, touring around the world, for over ten years, starting when they were teenagers.

Stepping forward, Kayden bumped fists with the drummer. "Hey, man. How're you?"

"Doing great. How are you?" the drummer asked. He was a dragon and occasionally while he was playing, he would tilt his head back and shoot flames up into the air. The crowd, myself included, loved it.

"Good. I'd like to introduce you to Princess Liliana of the Hybrids," he said and pushed my lower back to make me step closer.

"H-Hi. I'm a *huge* fan," I admitted nervously.

The drummer shook hands with me and smiled wide. He dipped his head in a quick bow once and said, "It's an honor to meet you, Your Highness. It means a lot to us that you're a fan."

"Would you guys sign this shirt for her?" Kayden asked and held out the shirt I'd asked for.

"Oh-Oh you don't have to, it's enough I got to meet you all," I said quickly.

"Anything for you, Kayden," the drummer said and took the shirt over to a table where they had a marker out.

Kayden introduced me to the other members and engaged in conversations with them like they were old friends. I envied him.

The bassist was a hybrid, like us, and clasped one of my hands in two of his as he bowed over them. "It is a great honor to meet you, Princess. I was an orphan and luckily adopted by one of the island hybrids you helped rescue. I know about your work with the orphanage and although it was after my time, I want to say how grateful I am to have a princess who is so kind."

My eyes watered but I blinked the tears away. "Thank you. I didn't know others knew about my work there."

"Only those of us who also help with the orphanage and orphans. We know you prefer to keep it quiet. I'd always hoped for a chance to meet you in person. Would you mind taking a selfie with me?"

"Yes, please!" I said a bit too loudly and stepped next to him. He put his arm around my shoulder, held out his phone, and just as he went to take the selfie, Kayden and the rest of the bandmembers stepped up to join us.

The crewmember who had brought us here took the phone and took the picture for us.

The bassist squeezed my shoulder. "Seriously, thank you for helping the orphans."

"As a fellow orphan who lucked into my home, I felt it was sort of my duty," I admitted.

Kayden sighed softly, but the singer distracted him with a question.

We sat down on the couches and they uploaded the image to their official social media account and tagged Kayden and I in it.

"Princess, how did you two meet?" the drummer asked.

"Oh, I've known Kayden since he was born. We're child-hood friends," I answered. "His dad used to be my guard."

"That's so sweet," the drummer said. "Sounds like me and my mate."

"How are your twins?" I asked, knowing they had posted about the twins being born less than a year ago.

"Growing like weeds," he said with a chuckle.

The crewmember whispered into the lead singer's ear and he nodded. "Unfortunately, we have to say goodbye for now so we can go perform. It was an honor to meet you, Your Highness, and great to see you again, Kayden. Text me next time you guys want to come to a concert and we'll hook you up."

"Thank you," I said, and they surprised me by each hugging both Kayden and I before we left.

"Did that really happen?" I asked him softly as we returned to our seats. I held up my concert t-shirt, signed by all of the members. I wasn't going to be able to wear it now. Instead, I would put it in a case and put it on my bedroom wall.

He thanked Bart, but whispered something in his ear that had him nodding before hurrying off.

Maybe he wanted another drink?

The band came out and everyone stood up, cheering.

To my surprise, they dedicated one of their songs to me and another to Kayden. And the thing Kayden had asked for was a second t-shirt so I could have one to wear. Turns out, he really did know me well.

I danced and sang along to all of the songs, having the most fun I'd had in years, and was truly happy without a hint of the darkness swirling within me.

"Yes, that all really happened," Kayden said during a quiet part of one of my favorite songs, answering me finally, and pinched me.

"Ouch," I hissed at him, but immediately smiled again, turned, and kissed him hard on the lips. "Thank you, Kayden."

He leaned over and rubbed his cheek along mine. "Anything for you, Lily."

SIXTEEN

Mom hovered over my shoulder as I continued fixing the spreadsheet she had destroyed the formulas for.

"You should really save these to the cloud so you have versions to allow you to restore a previous one to avoid this." I'd learned my lesson while at college after losing a ten-page essay and having to restart from scratch. I would never make that mistake again. I now anally hit save while working on important documents. This one included.

"I usually do, but the internet was down when I started it so I couldn't upload to the server."

"Well, lucky for you, I did several courses on electronic spreadsheets, including learning advanced coding." And as nerdy as that made me sound, I loved creating and editing spreadsheets. "Now after you enter the value here, when you hit enter, it will auto update on the other three tabs."

"You mean I don't have to enter it three separate times?" she asked, eyes wide.

I leaned back in the chair and nodded while smiling at her. "Exactly."

She threw her arms around me. "You are amazing! I'm so lucky you're my daughter. This will save me so much time!"

Laughing at her excitement, I patted her back. "I'm glad I could help." When I'd come into her office and found her sniffling, I had feared something awful had happened.

Riddick walked in with a binder in his hands. "How's it going?"

"She not only fixed it, but improved it!" Mom shouted.

Ge smiled proudly at me. "Wonderful! I know that spreadsheet has been annoying you the last month." He pressed a kiss to the top of her head and handed her the binder. "Quarterly report for the mana stone store. There's something interesting on it."

I double saved the spreadsheet to her desktop as well as the cloud, then got out of her chair so she could sit and review the report.

My eyes widened when I looked over her shoulder at the report. "A one hundred percent increase in sales? Why are so many people buying mana stones suddenly?"

"It increases as the demon portals increase," she explained. "People stocking up as a defense." Her brows furrowed as she looked at other pages of the report. "Who is the buyer that keeps purchasing the large quantities?"

"What?" Riddick asked.

I pointed to the row she mentioned where one person had purchased twenty mana stones once a week the entire quarter. "That's really suspicious. What could you possibly need that many for and that frequently?"

"You could power wards large enough for the city for a year with that," Mom whispered. "But not even this city has wards."

"I'll ask them for more information on the buyer," Riddick said and pulled out his phone to send a message.

"What are the dates of pickup?" I asked. "Maybe a stakeout would be better."

"You sound like Caleb," Mom muttered.

"And what's wrong with her sounding like me? Her father and king?" Dad asked as he walked inside. He wore a dark blue suit with a white shirt and matching blue tie.

"Whoa, you look like a businessman," I said. Dad preferred jeans to slacks.

"Had a TV interview today," he explained as he loosened his tie.

"There's a suspicious purchaser of the mana stones. Lily wants to do a stakeout."

His eyes sparkled as he smiled. "Oh, a stakeout, huh? I approve, as long as you take Kayden with you. Mason is too hotheaded for a non-confrontational stakeout."

"Why can't I go alone?" I asked with a scowl.

"I wouldn't let your mom go alone," he said quickly. "No way will I let you."

Mom stuck her tongue out at him. "Overprotective."

"What are we investigating anyway?" he asked and stepped up behind Mom to look at the report.

Riddick filled him in and Dad's face darkened.

"I don't like this at all," he whispered. "I'm going to call Nana Kara and see if she can think of any reason someone might need so many."

"The next pickup should be this evening," Riddick said as he read an email.

"Lily, I want you and Kayden to watch, scope the buyer out, but don't engage. Just find out who it is," Dad ordered me.

I pulled out my phone and dialed Kayden. "Okay," I agreed.

"What's up?" Kayden asked as he answered.

"I need you for a stakeout this evening. Can you meet me at the mana store at four o'clock? I'll fill you in then."

"Understood," he replied.

Ever the obedient soldier.

"You sure we should send Lily?" Mom whispered to Dad and Riddick.

"We are shorthanded and she's got a lot of free time," Dad said.

"And she volunteered," Riddick added.

"She came home to help the clan. This is one way for her to do that," Dad reminded Mom. "Plus, she's one of the best at suppressing her presence, so she's ideal for surveillance and recon."

"Even if her animal form is large," Riddick added, making them all snicker.

I lowered my phone and turned to glare at them. "I can hear you."

Dad and Riddick smiled, obviously aware.

"Well, since you have some time until your job tonight, how about you work on these other spreadsheets for me?" Mom said and opened three others on her computer. She stood and stretched. "I'm going to go buy lunch."

"I'll come with you," Riddick offered, linked hands with her, and opened the door.

Dad sat on the edge of the desk as I sat in the chair to get to work. "How is courting going? Did the trio provide a suitable explanation to you?"

I looked up at him and said, "Don't act like Ezio hasn't already filled you in."

He smirked. "He has, but he doesn't know how you feel about it and that's the most important piece. So, how do you feel, Lily?"

"Honestly, I'm a bit conflicted. Yes, their explanation makes sense and how it was a misunderstanding on my part. However, they could have come to see me. I know they were worried about finding me dating someone, but that feels like an excuse. I may have acted childish by trying to ignore them, but it felt like they ignored me for four years. I can't deny my attraction to them, they were my best friends, and when I'm with them it feels so ..."

"Effortless," Dad offered.

I nodded. "It feels like no time has passed, like we were never apart, and yet, my heart remembers the separation. Just once, if they had visited me just once, things would have been so different."

My hair glowed brighter the longer I spoke, but I wanted to get all the words out. Needed to.

"I can understand your feelings. You were with them most of your life and to suddenly lose them when you were also so far from home made it harder. However, you know the past can't be changed. You need to stop looking behind you and look at here and now and the future. Do you want to spend the next four years apart from them again? Could you handle seeing them mated to someone else?"

I hissed without thinking and quickly ducked my head.

Dad laughed and patted my head. "Pretty sure you've answered the question."

"So, accept them and move on? Just like that?" I asked and looked back up at him.

He shook his head. "No, make them grovel and show you how they really feel. Everyone who hurts their mate needs to grovel a bit. However, be honest with yourself about your feelings for them. Once they've groveled enough to please you, then accept their apology. Those boys could be knocked down a peg or two with little repercussions to their egos. But it might be enough for them to grow and become the type of mates you need. Don't tell them, but I've been secretly rooting for them since you were teens."

"It's really hard to stay mad at them when they're telling me sweet things like 'I'm the only one for them' and 'I'm what gets them through demon battles,'" I muttered and spun to face the computer again.

He laughed. "Well, they did grow up watching and listening to me and your other fathers apologizing and flirting with Ember a lot. Plus, Ezio made quite a few mistakes after Kayden was born."

"Ezio did?" I didn't remember them having issues.

"Mostly him not taking her feelings into consideration before doing things like taking on dangerous missions. He was so used to doing things on his own. Kayden, Mason, and Trey were surrounded by smooth-talking alphas who adore their mates. If they didn't pick up a few things, I'd be disappointed. I tried to beat a decent amount of respect for the women in our lives into them."

"So, you don't think it's an issue if they were basically groomed to wanting me as a mate?"

He rolled his eyes. "You are so like your mom. So self-deprecating. Those three have spent the last four years traveling around the world. They have met thousands of women. Had hundreds throw themselves at them and been forced on blind dates. They had ample time and other women at their call to decide you weren't the one for them. You know what happened instead? They realized you are their sun and no matter how hard those women tried to steer them off course, they came back to you because they love you. Because you are beautiful, kind, strong, sassy, and exactly what they want. Now, it's up to you to determine if the same is true for you. If you don't want them, end the courting now."

"Thanks, Dad."

He growled and ruffled my hair. "You're welcome."

I HAD JUST FINISHED MEDITATING when I sensed Kayden enter the store. He greeted the staff as he headed to the office where I waited.

His footsteps halted at the door and after a moment of hesitation, he opened it.

He wore black sweatpants and a black tank top, showing off his muscular arms. My eyes moved to his upper bicep where a snake tattoo wrapped around, red eyes bright on the otherwise white snake.

He had gotten my snake form tattooed on him, too?

Noticing my stare he said, "I got it just after you left for college."

"So, right before the incident?"

He lowered himself into the chair across the desk from me. "Yes."

"Regret it?" I asked.

"Yes, I regret not thinking how my words would be taken by you."

"I meant the tattoo."

He smirked, telling me he knew what I'd meant. "So, why are we staking out the store?"

I explained the reason and his brow furrowed.

"That is worrying. So, we're going to see who they are and report back to Caleb?"

I nodded. "They've been paying cash, so there's no name recorded."

"How do you want to do this? I can hide in fox form under a table. You're too large for that, no offense."

"I'm going to hide on top of the shelves."

The top of the shelves were over twelve feet high so I could lie on top of them in snake form without being spotted.

"I tested it earlier," I said quickly when his mouth popped open.

He closed his mouth and nodded. "Okay."

I stood and walked around the desk.

He stood and before I could open the door, he wrapped his arms around my waist and pressed his nose against my hair, inhaling deeply. "Did you have fun on our date last night?"

Turning around so I could look up at him, I smiled wide and nodded. "Thank you for taking me somewhere fun."

"Want to get some dinner after this?"

"I don't have any courting dates tonight, so that should be fine," I said and nodded.

"Now you do," he said, kissed me on the lips quickly, and opened the door.

One kiss and my body was on fire. I needed a cold shower.

Recomposing myself, I climbed the shelves, shifted, and got into position. I had my head in a perfect spot to see people as they approached the register, but without them able to see me.

Kayden triple checked that I was hidden before he shifted and hid under the table.

Emily, the one working today, would give us the signal when the person entered.

Thankfully, we only had to wait for an hour.

My scales warmed just below my jaw, making me worry that a demon portal had opened, but I didn't have time to check.

The door to the shop opened, the bell over it jingling in welcome.

"Good evening, sir. Are you here for your normal order?" Emily asked, the question our signal.

Peering over, I looked at the man walking up to the counter.

He was very unassuming, brown hair, brown eyes, no

alpha aura, nothing remarkable about him. Yet, there was something, a feeling, that he was a hybrid or someone I should know. Something ... familiar about him.

After getting his order, paying in cash again, he turned and headed out the door. For a split second, I thought he'd looked up at me, but his steps never faltered. His lip did quirk up as he pulled open the door.

Kayden suddenly rushed outside in fox form, just before the door closed.

I shifted as I slid off the shelves, landing on human feet.

Hurrying outside, I had to dodge people that were running away, down the sidewalk and lost his trail.

Worry made my heart race as I continued down the street, head on swivel as I tried to find Kayden and the source of all the people's fear.

The necklace warmed on my chest and I gripped it in one hand, following the pull into the next alley.

Kayden, still in fennec fox form, struggled in the grip of a huge boar-headed demon covered in shaggy gray fur. The demon was riddled with wounds and panting heavily.

Jumping forward, I drove my clenched fists down onto the bend of the demon's inner elbow, forcing him to release Kayden.

Kayden fell on human knees, sucking in a deep breath.

With a hard side kick, I sent the demon flying back through the portal right before it closed.

"Well, that was embarrassing," Kayden said after shifting into his human form.

"Are you okay?" I asked as I turned to face him.

He nodded. "I was following the man and saw him come

down this alley, but then the portal and demon were here. I don't know where the man went, if he went into one of the doors in the alley or through the portal."

My eyes widened. "You think he was a demon? He felt like a hybrid to me."

Kayden shrugged and dusted himself off. "He didn't look like a demon or feel like they do, but he was definitely suspicious. I'll call Caleb and update him while we head over to the restaurant."

"Oh, which restaurant?" I asked, shocked he still wanted to go to dinner.

"You choose, but I know you love the pasta place two blocks over." He pulled out his phone and we headed out of the alleyway.

"Princess, are you alright?" a male werewolf asked as we walked out.

I smiled at him. "Yes, thank you for your concern. I was able to force the demons back just as the portal closed."

He exhaled in relief. "Thank goodness you and Kayden were here. It makes me feel more at ease knowing you are focused on the demon problem."

I patted his shoulder as we walked by. "Just call in any portals or demons you see and we'll rush over."

He nodded vigorously.

Kayden filled in Dad about what had happened as we walked and I let my mind wander.

Could the demons be using the stones? If so, what for? It seemed odd for them to need them, but then again, we knew nothing about their world. There were a lot of uses for mana stones, not just for wards, but also to augment an individual's powers. Maybe that man was conducting experiments and needed the extra magic? Or maybe he was part of the demon problem and had used a spell to hide his identity? There were too many variables and questions without answers.

Dad said he'd have others do more stakeouts and try to find out who the mystery man was and told us to enjoy the rest of our night.

Kayden opened the restaurant's door for me and poked the middle of my forehead. "You keep scowling like that and you'll develop permanent wrinkles."

I rubbed the spot and stuck my tongue out at him. "Maybe I want wrinkles, then you'd forget all about our promise."

He slid his arm around my shoulders and squeezed me against his side. "I don't care if you're covered in wrinkles, scars, or whatever else. You're the only woman for me. You just need to accept that so you can stop these courting dates with men unworthy of you."

"Pretty conceited to think you're worthy," I whispered, though I didn't mean it.

"I know we aren't worthy of you either, but I'm too selfish and possessive to care."

And somehow those words made my heart flutter.

"Good evening, Your Highness. Allow me to escort you to the private room," the concierge greeted us with a warm smile.

"We can take a regular table," I said quickly.

"Nonsense, no one has reserved it anyway. Follow me," he said and hurried through the restaurant.

"She really is courting the demon trio," a man whispered as Kayden and I walked by.

"Lucky," a woman nearby muttered.

Kayden smirked down at me and I rolled my eyes at him.

We walked into the private room, an area sectioned off with walls to allow for conversations not to be overheard.

Once seated and drinks ordered, Kayden relaxed back against his seat and stared at me. "Your darkness seems to act up more frequently these days. Is it because of us? Do we agitate the darkness in you?"

I hadn't realized my hair was glowing until he said that. Embarrassed, I ducked my head and tried to calm myself. "It's just been an … eventful time."

"I think part of the problem is you haven't had enough *events* to cool your needs," he said and sipped on his water.

I choked on the water I'd been drinking, nearly spitting it out across the table.

Kayden just smiled wider.

"Was that an offer?" I asked back as I wiped my mouth, trying to regain some composure.

His eyes darkened and he leaned across the table to whisper, "Yes."

The door opened as our waiter returned with our drinks and I was glad for the interruption. My face, and body, were on fire as that one word made me squirm with need.

We ate mostly in silence, but the heat in my body would not dissipate. Kayden scowled and kept looking up at me, but didn't speak.

As we walked through the restaurant, he took a warrior shift of his wolf form.

"What?" I asked, looking around.

Everyone watched us, but of course they did when he shifted like that.

He put his arm around my shoulders and made me walk faster. "Let's head home," he said calmly in a gravely voice since he had shifted.

We stepped outside and I took a big breath of the cool night air. It still wasn't enough. I was still too hot. This had never happened before. Did I have a fever? Hybrids didn't usually get sick. Should I call Mom or Great Nana Kara?

I followed Kayden silently to his SUV that he'd parked near the mana stone store. I tried to open the passenger door, but he opened the back door instead.

I frowned in confusion, but climbed into the back, sliding onto the bench seat. The cool seat felt good against my hot skin.

Adding to my confusion, he climbed in with me. After locking the doors, he reached over and cupped my face with one hand. "There's absolutely no way I can drive like this. Not until I take care of you."

"What?" I asked, triply confused now.

He bent forward and licked the side of my neck, making me gasp and arch towards him. "You're practically choking me with your need. Had I been a weaker male, I'm certain I would have had to fight off several other males who smelled you as well. You are practically a beacon for males right now."

"I-I don't understand."

He slid a hand up my thigh and between my legs. "I've thought about hundreds of different ways of pleasuring you, about how our first time was going to be, but now, I'm going to have to forego my plans." Guiding me so I lay on my back on the seat, he pulled off my pants and immediately buried his face between my legs.

I moaned and gripped his hair.

Licking and sucking, he brought me to orgasm so quickly that I screamed and thrashed.

He held me down, forcing me to ride the orgasm out.

Leaning back, he pushed his sweatpants down, freeing his erection, and thrust into me, dropping one hand next to my head.

"This was *not* in my plan for tonight, but I think if I don't deal with your arousal now, I'm going to have to fight off a horde of alphas." He bent forward and nipped my ear, making me gasp and clutch at his shirt.

"So ... hot," I panted. "My body's ... on ... fire."

He nodded. "Your skin is practically burning mine. I've heard this happened to Jolie once. Don't worry, I've got you, Lily."

I matched his thrusts, fingers digging into his shoulder as the pressure built in my core. He was right, this wasn't normal for me.

I was glad he was with me though and that it was him, even if this was not how I expected our first time to go.

He peppered my face with gentle kisses, so at odds with his hard thrusts that I felt dizzy. Or, perhaps that was just this fever.

Sliding my fingers up his arms, I reveled at the muscles.

"You are so beautiful," he whispered as he continued to kiss me. "So perfect."

The darkness in my aura grew, my hair glowing with it, and I watched in shock as more of my darkness bled into Kayden's aura. I was too dizzy with need to draw back, though, or try to remove it.

Leaning back, he smiled at me and said, "Scream my name, Lily."

He shifted back, drawing my lower body up, and moving at a different angle that completely shattered me. I screamed his name as I came and just before he finished, he pulled out and came on the floor.

"Let's detour by the car wash before we go home," he said. "I need to clean that out as well as the scent evidence of what we've just done. Dad is supposed to use this SUV tomorrow and I don't think either of us wants to explain to him what happened."

I flushed, embarrassed. "No thank you."

He chuckled and dropped his face down, burying his nose against my neck. "Are you okay? It feels like your skin has cooled?"

I nodded. "Thank you."

He sat back and winked. "Anytime."

CHAPTER
SEVENTEEN

Nana Jolie and Great Aunt Leona sat across from me in Leona's house. Both were stone still after I explained everything to them about the darkness, the anger, the bloodlust, and the trio. My face burned as I explained what had happened yesterday with Kayden, but I needed to explain how I'd watched my darkness bleed into his aura.

I had left out the demons and the necklace, not wanting to admit anything about that for now.

After almost thirty seconds of silence, Nana Jolie leapt from her couch to mine and hugged me tight while petting my hair. "You poor thing! I can't believe you've kept this in for so long. Oh, baby!"

I would not cry. I would not cry. I would not cry!

She released me and Great Aunt Leona reached across to take one of my hands. "Sweetheart, I wish you had come to us sooner."

"Honestly, it was realizing the guys had been infected that really sent things over the edge for me."

"You've been struggling with this darkness on your own even though we told you to talk to us. Why?"

"It's very rare that it gets out of hand," I explained. "Like I said, I'm more worried about the guys."

"Well, we know your darkness isn't contagious or your family would have it as well," Great Aunt Leona said. "Jolie and I would have it with how much we interacted with you after you absorbed the spell."

Nana Jolie nodded her agreement.

"And the heat yesterday, that's something females experience sometimes when surrounded by males during highly fertile times. It's very rare to happen, but it can. You should be fine and not have to deal with it soon, but if you do, you definitely need to get away from any alphas you don't trust," Nana Jolie explained.

"Do you think there's a way to remove the darkness from the trio?" The chance it would change their feelings for me were high, but I would deal with whatever repercussions there were so long as they were safe.

"We need to inspect one of them," Nana Jolie said. "Do you know if any of them are available today?"

"I think they all went on a demon hunt this morning," I said and pulled out my phone to check the group chat they had started. They'd said the group chat was necessary so I could notify all of them if I encountered demons and needed their help. I hadn't argued. Messaging, I asked how the hunt was going. They immediately responded it was done and they were home. "They're all home," I answered.

"Let's ask them all to come so we can inspect each of

them," Nana Jolie said. She turned to Great Aunt Leona and asked, "Do you want us to do this somewhere else?"

She shook her head. "Here is fine."

"I'll text them," I said.

> Me: Can you come to Great Aunt Leona's?

> Mason: Demons?

> Me: No, not demons.

> Trey: Is something wrong?

> Me: That's what they want to determine.

> Kayden: We'll be there in twenty.

"They're on their way," I said, sighed, and leaned back with my eyes closed.

"You're worried they'll change how they feel about you?" Great Aunt Leona asked.

I nodded.

"We've known those boys their entire lives and I am pretty certain this won't change anything between you four," Nana Jolie said and patted my shoulder.

She didn't know that, but I appreciated her trying to ease my worry.

"Let me get some snacks," Great Aunt Leona said and went into the kitchen. "Anytime there are multiple alpha males, they need snacks or they get grumpy."

Keeping my eyes closed, I tried to stay calm and collected, to keep the darkness from activating at all.

Everything would be fine.

We would find a way to extract the darkness from the guys, they'd still be friends with me, and we'd move on with our lives with them in a better place.

We snacked on a charcuterie board of salami, cheeses, crackers, and some delicious jellies and mustards while we waited for the guys. It always amused me how simple snacks like this could be so enjoyable.

Kayden threw open the door and asked, "What's wrong?"

Great Aunt Leona rolled her eyes. "Always the dramatic one. Sit down and relax, Kay."

Kayden and Mason rushed over to sit on either side of me.

"I apologize for him barging in like that," Trey said and kissed them each on the cheek before he sat next to Kayden.

"We brought you here because Lily is worried that she somehow infected you guys with the darkness that she has from the spell she absorbed," Great Aunt Leona explained. She squinted her eyes, drew in a deep breath, and a second later, her eyes widened. "Well, you do have some, too."

"We've had it since we made the mating promise," Mason said.

Everyone turned to look at him.

"What?" Kayden asked.

"I can see auras. Not all the time, but when I try, and I noticed it appear after that night," he explained. Shrugging, he added, "Since it didn't change anything, I figured it was fine and didn't mention it."

Great Aunt Leona tapped her lips. "Interesting."

"We're going to have Lily try to extract it from you," Nana Jolie said.

"Why?" Mason asked. "If it doesn't harm us, why remove it?"

"Because it's not supposed to be there," I snapped. "Because it could have changed you without you realizing it if it happened that long ago."

"I have a theory," Kayden said. "What if you sharing the darkness with us, giving us part of it, is helping you deal with it since you don't have as much now?"

"How do I extract it?" I asked Nana Jolie, ignoring his theory.

"You have to consider it," Kayden said.

"You aren't supposed to have it, so it needs to be extracted," I said. "End of story."

"What if taking it back causes you to have more issues?" Trey asked.

"Then I'll deal with it."

"To extract it, you have to focus on the darkness in them, and the darkness in you, and pull theirs back into you. Imagine it drifting like smoke to you," Nana Jolie explained.

"Okay, let's try," I said and turned to Kayden.

"What if we don't want it extracted?" Mason asked. "What if we're fine holding it?"

Taking a deep, cleansing breath, I closed my eyes and focused on the darkness within me. Opening my eyes, I saw my hair was glowing and casting rainbows around the room. Eyes focused on Kayden's aura, I imagined his darkness drifting from him to me, to join the rest of it in my center.

His darkness swirled higher and higher, moving until all

of it was near his head. His eyes glowed a deep purple and his pupils became slitted, like snake eyes.

"Don't do it, Lily," he whispered. "I can feel how much it is. It's only going to hurt you to take on more."

"It was mine to begin with," I whispered back and imagined the smoke turning into a rope so I could pull it into me. Immediately, it all zipped out of him and into me, making me gasp and my back arch as it filled me. His darkness merged with mine and it swirled higher within me.

"How do you feel?" Nana Jolie asked Kayden.

He leaned back on the couch, staring up at the ceiling. "Lighter and also like I'm missing something at the same time." Clutching at his chest, he said, "Much calmer than I've felt in a long time."

"See," I whispered as I grit my teeth, "it changed you. You're not supposed to have it." Focusing on Trey, I said, "Your turn."

"Are you sure?" he asked with a scowl.

Instead of answering, I started the extraction process. When I pulled his from him, he moaned as he fell back against the couch. "So much lighter, but ... I feel like Kayden, that I'm missing something."

My teeth ground together and I had to close my eyes against the darkness surging within me, begging for an outlet already.

"Don't do it, Lily," Mason whispered and stood off the couch. "You're already glowing super bright and I can see you straining against it. I'm known as a loose cannon. Just let me keep mine. I don't care if it's altered my personality. I am who I am."

Opening my eyes, I looked at him and said, "You have the most of the three. At least double what the others had. You deserve to be who you are truly supposed to be. Who you should have been had I not infected you."

He knelt in front of me, took my face in his hands, and said, "I am who you need, and who you need is someone to help you deal with the darkness."

Setting my hands on top of his, I said, "I need you to be who you're supposed to be, Mason." Before he could pull out of my hold, I began extracting the darkness.

"No," he whispered as it slipped out of him. "Lily, stop. Please."

"Almost done," I whispered and grunted at the strain I felt trying to get his. There was so much in him and as I merged it with my own, I felt full of darkness. There was so much I didn't think I would be able to suppress it.

He whimpered as I released him.

Standing, I headed out of the house through the back-door. "Stay back!" I ordered everyone as I stumbled across the grass towards the field. I wanted blood, no *needed* blood. The more the better. Rivers of blood. A deep pulse thrummed within me, growing louder and louder by the second.

"Nana, shield around me!" I screamed.

"Lily, what's wrong?" Great Aunt Leona asked.

"It's going to explode," I gasped and clutched at my chest, trying to keep it inside of me, but I knew it was in vain. "Nana! Shield!" If she didn't put a shield around me, I wasn't sure what would happen to anyone who got hit with the blast.

"Give it back!" Mason shouted. "Give it back to us so we can help you!"

I shook my head and continued to stumble away from them, trying to get farther away.

Mason tried to follow me, but Great Aunt Leona grabbed his arm, stopping him.

Nana Jolie put the shield around me, a translucent bubble that would keep others from getting to me and would contain the power. "Are you sure, Lily? Are you sure you don't need something else? What if it hurts you?"

It was possible the power exploding out of me would hurt me, I knew that, but there was no other way.

Mom teleported into the yard, surveyed the situation, and asked, "What's going on?"

"She took it from us," Mason snarled. "She took it and now it's going to hurt her! Give it back, Lily!"

"She said it feels like it's going to explode," Nana Jolie informed Mom.

Dropping to my knees, clutching at my chest, I could barely breathe. My heart hammered in my chest and my lungs ached for more air. The pressure from the darkness built higher and higher, spreading all throughout my body. Looking at my arms, I could see it leaking out of me, like steam off my skin. There was so much darkness in the shield that I couldn't see out of it anymore.

"Lily!" Mason, Kayden, and Trey screamed.

The build reached a crescendo and I screamed as it exploded outward. A feeling of weightlessness filled me, a sensation of being underwater.

Darkness surrounded me, pulsed within me, was me.

I was the darkness. The darkness was me. One and the same.

Someone pounded on the shield around me, several voices screamed, but I couldn't understand any of it.

My necklace warmed against my chest.

"Accept the darkness," a deep, unfamiliar voice said. "Accept it and make it yours. Once you've made it yours, forced it to accept you as the one in charge, you won't have to fear it. Once it's yours, you will be its master and it will do as you order."

"Who are you?" I asked.

"A friend," the voice replied. "Now, accept it, force it to submit to you. Become the person you are supposed to be."

"Who is that?"

"A goddess," the voice whispered.

The necklace cooled and the cool feeling gave me a bit more control.

Doing as they said took a lot longer than I liked, but once I got the power under control, I was able to absorb it back and extinguish it.

With the smoke gone, I could see out of the shield.

Trey, Mason, and Kayden were on their knees in front of the shield, staring inside. All three looked terrified.

Grandpa Nico, Mom, Caleb, Riddick, Triston, Branson, Nana Jolie, Great Aunt Leona, and Great Uncle Silverowl all stood around the shield as well.

Getting to my feet, I stretched my arms out to my side, drew in a deep breath, and summoned the darkness. It swirled and wrapped around my arms and morphed into a black smoke snake with red eyes. The smoke snake looked at me with reverence. "You will do as I say," I told it.

The snake dipped its head in acknowledgment.

Closing my fist, the snake disappeared, the darkness went back within me, swirling in my body, but calmly, and I realized I no longer felt the bloodlust like I normally did when it was moving within me.

Looking up at the trio, I smiled and said, "New power unlocked."

CHAPTER
EIGHTEEN

Once they were sure I was safe, they removed the shield and ran to me. Everyone, but the trio.

Mason turned his back on me, shifted into his raven form, and flew away.

"Give them some time to adjust," Nana Jolie whispered as she hugged me. "Having it removed and thinking you were about to die is a lot to deal with."

I nodded and hugged her back. "Thank you for listening to me."

She laughed softly. "I've learned that if someone calls for a shield like that, it's to protect others and it's best to listen."

Mom pulled me into a tight hug. "You scared me."

"I'm sorry," I whispered as I hugged her back. "I was scared, too."

"Who were you talking to?" Kayden asked.

Shit, they'd heard that?

"I don't know," I admitted. "They told me to make the

power mine and that they were a friend. I've never heard the voice before, though."

Should I tell them about the necklace warming? Was it related somehow? I felt like it was something I shouldn't bring up.

"Did they say anything else?" Caleb asked.

"That I was becoming the person I am supposed to be. To be a goddess," I admitted.

"A goddess?" Mom asked with a frown and turned to Nana Jolie. "Have you heard anything like that before?"

"We were taught about goddesses and gods, but it was mythology, not real," Nana Jolie said. "Or, so we thought."

"It could still be mythology," Caleb said. "She doesn't look like she's changed." At my frown, he smiled and said, "No offense, cub."

"It's likely bullshit," I said and shrugged. "However, their advice did help, so I'm grateful even if I don't know who they are."

"Maybe the darkness wasn't related to the spell at all," Mom suggested. "Maybe it was a coincidence, like the personality altering spell woke up the darkness that was already in her. I don't even think darkness is an appropriate term for it, honestly."

"We'll do some research," Grandpa Nico said to me and patted my shoulder.

Turning to Kayden and Trey, I asked, "How are you feeling? Better?"

I stepped closer to them, but when they tensed, I stopped.

"It's ... complicated," Kayden answered. "If you're okay, we're going to head out to find Mason."

"Oh, sure," I said and wrapped my arms around myself. Had it changed how they felt about me?

"We're glad you're okay," Trey said and gave me a tense smile.

I nodded. "I'll text you about our dates, okay?"

They nodded and walked away.

Nana Jolie put her arm around my shoulder and squeezed. "Give them a day of breathing room. It's not always easy dealing with such a sudden change."

"Okay," I whispered.

"Let's get you home," Mom said and pulled me out of Nana Jolie's hold. She teleported us to the house and I immediately went up to my room to shower.

Although I felt better, stronger and more powerful, than ever, I felt like something was missing. Was this missing piece what the guys were talking about? On top of that was my concern over Mason and how the guys were reacting. Would Mason forgive me? Would this change our dynamic like I'd been worried it would?

I supposed only time would tell.

Once out of the shower, I messaged Great Nana Kara about the elf girl who shifted into a snake to set up a time to go see her and try to help. Drying my hair with the towel, I flopped onto my bed and sighed at the framed concert t-shirt with a print of the picture with the band. Why did that feel like it was a year ago when it had just happened yesterday?

Sitting up, I went to my desk, grabbed the calendar book, and flopped back onto my bed to message Liam for a second date. I'd wait to message the trio for theirs until I'd given them at least a day to decompress.

Liam replied almost immediately accepting my first offered date of one week from now. He promised to think of something fun and would message me details the day before.

Setting my phone on the bed beside me, I closed my eyes.

Two knocks on my door had me up and eyes open.

Tony stuck his head in and smiled. "Hey, Sis." His body was tense, so I opened my arms and he immediately ran forward to hug me, resting his head on my shoulder. "You okay?"

"Yes and no," I admitted with a humorless laugh.

"Mom told me what happened. I'm sorry I couldn't be there to help you."

Tsking, I said, "What could you have done, little bro? It all worked out in the end."

Pushing me back he asked, "Do you want ice cream?"

Scoffing, I rolled my eyes, and said, "Well, I'm not here to fuck spiders."

He sighed and shook his head, hating the saying I had picked up from a fiction novel I'd read. It basically meant, "duh, what else would I be here for?"

"Mom already has the ice cream and toppings out, so we better hurry or dads are going to eat it all."

I gasped and pushed him towards the door. "Why didn't you lead with that? They're going to eat all the cherries!"

Laughing, we ran down the stairs and to the kitchen where everyone was making bowls of ice cream. This was a sort of family tradition. If something crazy or emotionally draining happened, we would have build-your-own-sundaes and only talk about fun or funny things.

"Don't eat all the cherries!" I yelled as I ran into the kitchen, my socks sliding on the tile.

"I saved the last two for you," Branson said.

"You're the best, Bran Bran!" I shouted as I ran around to where he was and grabbed them from the little cup he'd put them in.

Once our sundaes were made, we made our way to the living room and I gasped when I saw one of my favorite board games on the table. "I didn't know we still had this!"

"It was in the back of the cupboard," Riddick said. "I had to dig it out."

"Oh, you guys are going to get destroyed!" I said confidently.

"While you were at college, I became the reigning champion," Tony said proudly.

"Yeah, while I was gone," I scoffed. Pulling out the board and the pieces, I started assembling it.

Four hours later, I reclaimed my title as reigning champion by winning seven games in a row.

"How does she do it?" Tony asked, exasperated. "I swear she cheats somehow."

"I don't cheat. I'm just that good," I taunted.

He jumped at me in his wolf form and I shifted into my snake form, coiling around him, but not squeezing tight enough to hurt him.

"Whoa, you are much bigger," Caleb said.

Tony huffed and relaxed, his way of telling me that I won, so I uncoiled and shifted into my human form.

"Yeah, I haven't measured myself, but I feel like I've grown at least a foot," I said.

"Let's measure you," Triston said and stood immediately.

"You just don't want to get beaten at the game again," I teased.

He smiled, clicked his tongue, and pointed at me. "Right you are. Now, let's go measure you."

Out in the barn, there was a doorframe that they'd used to mark our heights and a wall that they used to mark our animals' sizes.

I stopped at the doorframe first, but neither Tony or I had changed since last year. Shifting into my snake form, I put my head at the beginning of the wall, in the corner, and spread my body down the wall until everything was against the wall and the tip of my tail was as long as I could make it.

"Whoa," Triston said, "you've grown over a foot for sure. You can shift back now, I marked it. Branson get the tape measure."

Shifting and walking over to him, my mouth dropped open at the difference from the previous mark to this one. "Whoa."

"That's what I said." Triston chuckled.

Tony held the end of the tape while Branson walked down the wall until he reached us and read, "Twenty feet and three inches."

"That's two feet," Riddick said behind us. "That's quite a growth spurt, Lily."

"Well, the research we did said she'd likely reach full maturity this year or next," Mom commented. "So, it's not too surprising she grew more, but that is a lot. Did you shed?"

I nodded. "Twice this year, which was abnormal, but I thought it was from the stress of trying to finish the school year."

"I think we have to upgrade your rock and pool," Caleb commented and we all turned to look at it.

"I still fit," I said, shifted, and slid my way over to the rock, curling up on it to prove my point.

Mom shook her head. "You fit, but barely. I think a bigger one would be better."

I slid into the pool and sighed at the cool water. I quickly realized that it was a bit too small and if I put my head just outside of it and draped my body across of the pond like I liked, at least a foot of my tail stuck out.

"Yeah, we need to dig that bigger as well," Branson said.

Climbing out of the water, I shifted, and pouted. "Sorry."

"Don't apologize for something you can't control, Lily," Mom chastised me.

"It'll only take us an afternoon to dig your pool larger," Branson said. "It's not a big deal."

"And I think I know a rock about three miles north that should be big enough to replace this one," Caleb said. "Tony and I can go out and we should be able to carry it."

"I'll go with you in case you need help carrying it," Riddick offered.

"Should you really go through all that trouble if I'm likely to end up mated soon ... ish?"

"Are you planning to never visit us when you get mated? Just going to act like we don't exist and stop visiting your clan?" Caleb asked and folded his arms over his chest.

I rolled my eyes. "Of course not."

He dropped his arms and smiled. "Then, it's perfectly reasonable for us to make a space for you that you'll enjoy."

"That's what family does," Tony said and hugged me one armed.

"Speaking of family," Mom said as she pulled her ringing phone from her pocket. "It's Kara. Hello?" Her eyes widened and she looked at me. "We'll be right there." She hung up, marched over, and grabbed my shoulder. "We have to go help the snake shifter. She's trying to eat something and it's stuck in her throat."

"Let's go," I agreed with a nod.

She teleported us to Great Nana Kara's house in the elven territory.

"Where?" I asked.

"I'll lead you," Great Uncle Silverowl said, walked out of the house, and shifted into his owl form. I ran just behind him, letting him lead the way.

We ran towards a group of homes and I saw people in a semi-circle.

Rushing forward, I slid on my knees towards the four-foot-long python with a deer halfway swallowed.

She thrashed on the ground, eyes wide in panic.

"Easy," I whispered and set my hand on her head. "I'm a snake shifter, too, I'm Princess Liliana. Let me look at you and see if I can help."

She blinked her eyes at me and stopped thrashing.

Tilting her head, I realized her breathing tube was stuck between a hoof and the deer's body, making it hard for her to breathe.

"I'm going to help free your breathing tube, okay? You understand?"

The little snake bobbed its head as much as it could.

Reaching down, I freed her breathing tube and watched her take a big breath. Stroking her head, I smiled. "There you go, pretty girl." I admired her brown and black scales with a bit of red. "Your scales are gorgeous. I'm going to leave you to finish feeding, but after you've digested your meal, I'll come visit you again, okay?"

She took another swallow of the deer, being careful to keep her breathing tube out, and nodded again.

Standing, I turned to the two teary-eyed elven parents. "She'll be okay now. I'm sure that was scary for you."

The mom threw her arms around my shoulders and hugged me tight. "Thank you! Thank you so much! We didn't know what to do."

I patted her back and smiled at the father. "It's okay. It's something that you learn as you get older, so it's understandable this happened. I'll come back and teach her more after she's digested this meal. Don't move her from here for at least two days, okay? We can move, but it's really uncomfortable to be moved while we're digesting. Don't be surprised if it takes her a week or more to digest that, too. I'm not sure how quick her digestion is, as I only have myself as a sample."

"Thank you," the father said and gripped my hands. "We're in your debt, Princess."

"Nonsense," I said and shook my head. "That's part of what I'm here for." I gave them my phone number and told them to call once she'd finished digesting.

Great Uncle Silverowl put his arm around my shoulders

and squeezed as we headed back towards the main house. "I'm glad you were able to realize the issue so quickly."

"Well, let's just say I might have experienced something similar when I was little. I didn't realize the true issue because Tony had pulled the animal I was swallowing partially out of my throat, allowing the tube to be freed, but after some research, I realized my error. After that, I did a ton of research on reticulated pythons so I knew more about myself."

"I'm sorry we don't have much information on your kind of shifter," he whispered. "I'll do more research myself to ensure we can help her as she grows."

I leaned my head against his shoulder and said, "As long as she has someone understanding and accepting like you, Great Uncle, she'll be fine."

"Is everything okay?" Great Nana Kara asked and stood as we entered the house.

"Yes," Great Uncle Silverowl answered. "Lily was able to help the girl and everything is fine now."

"Breathing tube," I told Mom.

She exhaled loudly and sagged her shoulders. "Those poor parents must have been terrified. I remember Tony telling me about that."

I nodded. "It is scary, especially as the snake. I knew I couldn't shift with half of an animal in my mouth and I couldn't breathe. If Tony hadn't helped, I might have suffocated."

Mom hugged me and growled.

"Mom, that was like two decades ago," I whispered with my face pressed against her chest.

She released me after one more squeeze. "Are you ready to return home?" she asked.

"Wait," Great Nana Kara said and walked up to me. She reached a hand out, set it on my chest, and closed her eyes while drawing in a deep breath. "Something's changed in you."

"Oh, uh, yeah," I said, unsure if we should tell her what had happened. I glanced at Mom who shrugged one shoulder.

"I don't know what you did, but you're definitely more stable now," Great Nana Kara said, opened her eyes, and smiled up at me.

"Let's hope it stays that way," I said with a nervous laugh.

"Come on, let's get home before your dads start worrying," Mom said.

"Thank you for your help," Great Uncle Silverowl said.

"Bye!" I said and waved to the two of them before Mom teleported us. I held up my hand as all of my dads and Tony asked questions. "Mom can explain. I'm going for a walk before bed."

"Stay in the wards," Mom ordered me.

I waved my hand dismissively at her as I walked away, even though I definitely would stay in the wards. Heading out the back door, I walked through the woods I'd grown up in, woods that were as much my home as the house behind me.

Closing my eyes, I trailed my fingers along the trees, drawing in deep breaths of the delicious forest scents.

My mind drifted to Mason, Trey, and Kayden. They'd spent as much time in these woods as I had and were often on my mind when here. Would their fighting abilities change without the darkness in them? Without that additional bloodlust?

My chest hurt to consider they might no longer feel as strongly as they used to, that those statements of loyalty might be void now.

The necklace warmed on my chest and a portal opened a few feet away from me.

I shifted into a warrior form, crouched down, and waited for whatever was going to come out.

A small hellhound, no larger than a loaf of bread, ran out of the portal whining and yelping, its tail tucked between its legs. It ran towards me, then ducked behind my leg.

Staring in utter disbelief, I realized it was hiding behind me.

Out of the portal, two large hellhounds walked out, snarling and drooling.

The little hellhound whimpered and cowered into a small ball behind my leg.

Clearly, it was scared of these larger hellhounds, and while the trio would likely tell me to just kill the hellhound for being a hellhound, I couldn't bring myself to do it. The little thing was obviously a baby and didn't seem to want to hurt me.

"Go back through the portal," I ordered the big hellhounds.

They continued towards us and snapped their teeth. The pup ran farther away from the portal, hiding behind a tree.

The two hounds tried to run past me and towards the pup.

"Fine, have it your way," I said and jumped into their path, smacking them away from the pup and back towards the portal with my tail.

After getting back to their feet, they jumped apart, and tried to attack me from different sides.

Tony and Caleb ran forward, each focusing on a different hellhound.

"How many?" Caleb asked.

"Just these two so far," I said, not wanting to tell them about the pup.

They quickly killed the two hellhounds and stepped back to stand beside me as we all faced the portal, waiting for something else to come out.

"I still smell them," Tony commented and raised his nose. "Is it just because their bodies are here?"

My eyes darted to the pup who was looking at me with wide, scared eyes. "Y-Yeah, that must be it," I said quickly and looked away so they wouldn't look in the direction I was.

Kayden and Mason ran over, eyes wide at the two dead hellhounds.

"Everyone okay?" Mason asked. His eyes skimmed over me, but quickly focused on Caleb.

My heart clenched and I took a step back.

"Yes, we're fine," Tony answered.

Kayden glanced at me then back at the portal and back to me again.

"I didn't try to go through it," I snapped and turned away from him. "It opened in front of me and I fought the hellhounds, then Dad and Tony showed up. That's all."

"I didn't say anything," he muttered.

"You didn't have to," I hissed and shifted into my human form.

The portal closed, the necklace cooled, and I took a deep breath to slow my heart.

"We'll leave you to your walk," Caleb said. "We just wanted to make sure you were safe since we sensed the ward break."

"Thanks, I'm good. You can all leave now," I said, still not looking at them.

Dad and Tony headed back towards the house, but Kayden and Mason lingered.

After another second, they walked away as well.

The little pup stuck its head out from behind the tree and looked at me.

"Yes, the coast is clear," I told it and squatted down with my hand out.

Slowly, tail still tucked beneath itself, the pup walked to me and sniffed my hand. Its quills were black with a red tip, the eyes were odd and looked smoke-like, and yet was still very expressive. The pup looked up at me, raised its tail, ears perked up, and barked. The little tongue lulled out the side of its mouth as it wagged its tail at me.

"I'm not sure what to do about you, pup. I didn't show the others, but they'll smell you for sure. How do I know you won't grow big and try to kill me in my sleep or something?"

It canted its head, sat on his rump, and continued panting with its tongue hanging out one side of its mouth.

Groaning, I said, "You're just too cute!" Reaching out again, I ran my hand down the top of its head, surprised that the quills felt almost furlike when stroked in this direction.

Using my nail, I lifted one and looked at the sharp tip. "These definitely don't feel good when going the opposite way."

It whoofed softly and wagged its tail more.

Sighing, I put my face in my hand and muttered, "What have you gotten yourself into, Lily?"

The pup rubbed its head on my hand and licked it.

"Fuck, you're too cute. I can't let them kill you," I grumbled. Pointing my finger at it, I said, "You have to do exactly what I say, you understand?"

It woofed, stood, and wagged its tail harder.

"Come on, let's go to the barn. It'll be easier to hide you there than in my room, since my parents don't go into the barn often. Plus, they'd hear you in the house and definitely smell you easier there."

Walking towards the barn, I was pleased to see the pup trotting next to me, ears perked and tail up, ridiculous tongue still out the side of its mouth.

Shaking my head, I said, "Don't make me regret this, pup."

In response, it looked up at me with adorable puppy eyes and woofed again.

I was so screwed.

CHAPTER
NINETEEN

Turned out the pup could eat meat and snored softly when it slept. I convinced my family that I wanted to stay in the barn because I'd neglected shifting while at college, so I wanted to refamiliarize myself with my snake form and spend a lot of time in it.

The pup listened to my instructions with an above average intelligence and anytime someone from my family came to visit me, he would run and hide behind a crate I'd put behind my rock for that very purpose.

I crafted a carrying bag for him since his quills hurt when I tried to hold him. He loved the bag, curling up inside and huffing a soft, contented sigh each time I put him in it.

And I had confirmed the pup was male after watching him pee a few times.

Going out deep into our territory, far enough that I knew I wouldn't be interrupted, I brought a notepad and snacks for some experiments.

"Let's see how smart you are," I said to the pup. "Can you do a flip?"

The pup climbed out of the bag, walked a little away, and did a backflip.

I tossed him a piece of jerky. "Good job!"

It swallowed the jerky and barked happily.

"Can you count? If I tell you to count to three, can you claw the ground three times?"

His head canted to the side, tongue back in his mouth, obviously confused.

Making a note in my notepad I said, "Okay, can't count."

A butterfly flew by and his head whipped up, following the butterfly. The butterfly flew right over and landed on the pup's snout.

Fumbling, I pulled my phone out of my pocket and snapped a picture. "Oh, my goodness. That was adorable!"

The next second, the pup snapped its jaws and swallowed the butterfly.

Sighing, I shook my head and lowered my phone. "I should have guessed that would be your next move. You remind me of my brother when he was a pup. He used to eat butterflies, too." Leaning my elbows on my crossed knees, I set my head in my hands and pondered the pup. "Why were those adult hellhounds after you? Did you do something wrong?"

The pup chased after a grasshopper, ignoring my questions.

"Do you want to go home? Back through a portal?" I asked him.

His head whipped around and he barked several times as he ran around me.

Laughing, I said, "I guess that's a yes. We just have to find the perfect place."

"Who are you talking to?" Mason asked behind me.

I yelped, grabbed the bag, and opened it so the pup could run inside. He did so immediately, curling up as small as he could. "Um, myself," I said, stood, and turned to face him, putting my closed legs in front of the bag to hide it.

Mason scowled at me and looked at my snacks and notepad. "Why are you so far from the house?"

"I wanted some alone time to think," I said, which was partly true.

He took a step back. "Sorry for intruding."

Reaching a hand out towards him, I said, "Wait! Mason, you don't have to leave. I just ..."

"I'm actually just on a perimeter run, but thought I scented demons and knew I scented you, so I wanted to check," he said.

"Well, no demons here," I said and laughed, but the laugh came out awkward.

He nodded. "Right. Well, I better complete my run."

"O-Okay," I said.

Before I could say more, he shifted into his bird form and flew off.

Sitting back down, I huffed. "Well, that didn't go well."

The pup poked his head out and when he saw we were alone, then crawled out to sit before me.

Touching the necklace, I wondered if it were possible to summon or track down a portal with it to return the pup.

"I think we need to go on a trip," I told him. "To find a portal for you."

Grabbing the bag, I tapped it. "Come on, inside."

The pup hopped into the bag and curled up into a tiny, prickly ball. After gathering the rest of my items, I made the trek back to the house to grab my purse before heading towards the garage. Voices around the corner of the house, had me freezing to listen.

"I'm telling you, I smell a demon and it gets stronger the closer to her that I get," Mason whispered.

"Are you trying to tell me that you think she's a demon now?" Tony asked and scoffed.

"No, I think maybe she's possessed by one. She said she heard a voice tell her how to handle the darkness, remember?"

"You used to have that darkness in you, did you feel like you were possessed?" Tony asked back.

"At times, it felt like that, honestly," Kayden said.

"I would know if she were possessed," Tony said. "I've been spending time with her each day and while she does smell different, she's not acting different. Actually, this is the most like her that she's been since before she left for college."

"Something is off," Mason said sternly.

"What's off is that you two haven't reached out to her since she took the darkness from you. Are you trying to ruin your chance at mating with her?" Tony snapped.

"Mating isn't what's important right now. Figuring out why she stinks of demon is," Mason snapped back.

Rolling my eyes, I backed up several feet, then started skipping and humming as I passed the house and continued towards the garage. I smiled and waved to the three of them as I passed. "Bye! I'm going into town. I'll be back later!"

"Don't you need a guard?" Kayden asked.

"You going to guard me?" I asked him back.

When he blinked at me, I waved my hand dismissively. "No, I'm fine. I'll scream for help like a damsel in distress so some other big, strong alpha can save me. Might help me find another person who wants to court me." I shrugged and gave them another smile over my shoulder as I opened the garage and went inside, smiling at the growl Mason and Kayden had made at my taunt.

Quickly, before they could ask to join, I started one of the cars and headed out of the territory. I didn't have my own car because I hadn't been home and preferred not to drive, but since we had so many cars, I always had one available to borrow.

The pup snored softly in the passenger seat inside of the bag, which made me laugh at the cuteness.

It still bothered me that the adult hounds had clearly been chasing him and I had no idea why. I hoped sending him back wouldn't be sending him to his death.

Keeping one hand on the necklace, I drove slowly around the city, knowing the portals most commonly happened in highly populated areas.

The park had been a location twice, but I wasn't sure if it would happen a third time or if that was the extent of times it would show up there.

"Come on," I whispered. "Give me an empty portal so I can send the little rascal home."

A thought occurred to me. I could buy a burner phone, set it to videocall myself, and attach it to the pup as I sent him through. It wasn't quite the same plan as what I'd told the guys, but it also meant I wouldn't have to try to put the phone through myself.

"Quick stop," I whispered as I turned down the next street to head to a store that sold phones. Parking in front of the store, I debated if I should take the pup or leave him. If he happened to get out of the bag while I was in the store, it could spell disaster for me.

Opening the bag a bit, I peeked inside and said, "You stay here, in the bag, until I get back. Do you understand?"

He barked softly and curled back up with his tail over his eyes. I closed the bag, gnawed nervously on my lip again, and hurried out of the car. The faster I got the phone, the faster I could get back to the car.

Luckily, there was a hat in the car, one of Tony's, so I shoved my hair inside of it, pulled the bill down to cover my face as much as I could while also looking down, and hurried inside of the store.

"Good afternoon!" the store owner called out.

Rushing to the phones, I grabbed the cheapest one, grabbed a card to add three hours of call time, ran to the accessories, and grabbed a waterproof bag that had a draw-string I could secure the phone to the pup with. "Just these," I said and pulled out my credit card.

The owner scanned the items and put them inside of a bag. "Do you need anything else?" he asked, looked at my card, and gasped. "Y-Your Highness."

"Shh," I urged him and glanced up. "Please, I'm in a hurry."

He tapped the screen on his register to get the receipt and held the bag out, hands shaking, and bowed. "Thank you for your patronage."

"Thank you," I said, grabbed it and my card, and ran out of the store and to my car.

Looking over, I was relieved to see the bag still there, opening it, the pup peeked at me, huffed, and put its tail back over its eyes.

"Phew," I whispered and set the bag of items on the passenger floorboard.

"Why the hurry?" Mason asked behind me.

I screamed and partially shifted.

The pup in the bag yelped in fear and started shivering.

Mason's eyes narrowed on the bag. "What—"

He started to reach for it and I knocked his hand away. "Don't touch him!"

His eyes widened. "Him? What is in the bag, Lily?" Eyes narrowing, he asked, "Is this your child?"

Barking out a quick laugh I asked, "Is that really what you think of me, Mas? That I'd get knocked up, not tell anyone, and then have it somewhere secretly? Wow."

"No, I don't think you'd do that, but you've been acting incredibly suspicious and there's obviously something going on." He indicated the bag.

Exhaling softly, I said, "If I tell you, you have to promise, swear to me, that you won't harm him."

He leaned back in the back seat and folded his arms across his chest. "Why do I get the feeling you're making me swear that because it needs to be killed."

"Shush!" I hissed and looked at the bag that was quivering in fear now. "Just ... just promise me."

He sighed and rubbed his eyes. "Fine, I promise I won't kill whatever it is when you show me it."

"Or after!" I snapped.

He sighed again. "I won't kill it unless it attacks me or you. Happy?"

"No, but I suppose that's the best I'm going to get with you." Taking a deep breath, I said, "It's a hellhound pup."

"What!" Mason bellowed and drew his sword. "Lily, that is not—"

"You promised!" I shouted.

He clenched his sword and stared at the bag.

"Just ... just let me find a portal so I can send him back. Okay? That's what I'm doing. I'm trying to find a portal so he can go home."

His eyes widened and his sword lowered. "That's what you meant when you said, 'the perfect place?'"

I nodded.

"How long have you had it?" he asked.

"A few days," I admitted.

He chuckled, but there was no humor in the laugh.

"I'm going to put together the thing I bought and resume driving, okay?"

He shook his head. "Let me drive. You and the *pup* can ride in the back, put your thing together, and give me directions."

Carefully, I grabbed the pup's bag and the new bag, and got out of the car, climbing into the bag seat to do as he'd said.

Mason, true to his word, got into the driver's seat and started driving.

"Aren't you going to ask how I can sense the portals?" I asked him as I turned the phone on, adding the time to it, and set it up so it could do a videocall with me.

"If you wanted to tell me, you would have," he said.

"Where did you guys get this necklace?" I asked as I unpackaged the waterproof case next.

"We found it during a demon hunt," he answered and glanced up at me in the rearview mirror. "The necklace?"

I nodded. "It warms when there's a portal opening or a demon nearby."

He cursed and looked out the side window. "I knew it felt weird, but they wouldn't listen to me. They thought it was something one of the demons had grabbed and when we killed it, dropped it, so it was a spoil of war. They said it would be a great mating gift for you, a reminder of why we had been separated, but that we were always thinking of you."

When he put it like that, it was a thoughtful gift.

"It is beautiful," I said and stroked a finger down the gem.

"You should take it off."

"I ... can't."

He hit the brakes a bit hard and I had to put my arm out to keep the pup's bag from sliding off. Whipping around to face me he asked, "What?"

"I can't take it off. I tried and I physically can't do it." Opening the bag, I smiled at the scared pup. "Don't worry, Mason may hit the brakes hard, but he's an excellent driver."

The pup yipped and thumped its tail inside the bag.

"Let me try to take it off for you," Mason said and reached between the front two seats.

I batted his hand away. "Not yet. I need it to get him home."

He growled, but sat back down and turned around.

"I'm going to take him out of the bag so I can attach something to him. Don't growl at him or freak out, okay?"

Mason exhaled through his nose and continued driving.

Carefully, I put the cord of the waterproof bag around the pup's neck and tightened it.

The pup groaned and shook his head.

"Keep it on for me at least a little bit after you get through the portal we find, okay?"

The pup sighed and laid down, ears flattened to his head, in an adorable sulk.

"Good boy," I praised.

"Wish she'd call me that," Mason whispered. I was definitely not meant to hear it, but it made me curious what he would do if I did say it to him.

Putting the phone into the case, I prepared it for the videocall.

"Okay! Now we just need to find a portal!" My chest immediately warmed from the necklace. "Pull over!" I gasped.

Mason swerved to the right and parked the car. "Where?" he asked, looking around.

We were in a warehouse area and there didn't appear to be many people around, which was perfect for my plan.

"Alright, little buddy, I'm going to keep you in the bag

until it's time for you to run through a portal to get home, okay?"

The pup yipped, wagged his tail, and jumped into the bag.

I started the videocall with my phone, activated the screen recording app, and set it to auto-upload the recording to my cloud server.

Grabbing his bag, I hurried out of the car and followed the necklace to the portal. It led us around the nearest warehouse, to the back area, where we had to climb up and over a chain link fence.

Mason stayed at my side with his sword drawn.

"Where do you keep that thing? I swear it's invisible until you draw it," I whispered as we neared the portal's location.

"The scabbard is enchanted to be invisible until I touch the sword's hilt," he said.

"I knew it," I whispered.

The portal came into view and it looked like it was empty.

Mason walked out first, checked nothing had come through that we could see, and waved me forward.

I set the bag on the ground and opened it so the pup could climb out. "Alright, pup, it's time for you to go home."

He wagged his tail, jumped up to lick my cheek, and ran through the portal.

Pulling out my phone, I stared, wide-eyed at my phone screen.

"What's that?" Mason asked as he looked over my shoulder.

"The demon world," I whispered.

As the pup ran, he stopped atop a large rock, showing us a world of blackened dirt and what looked like burned trees. In the distance was a tall spire.

Squinting to try to see it better, I asked, "Is that a castle?"

Mason leaned in closer, but the next second, the pup yelped and took off, running and whining in fear.

When he looked behind him, we saw what he was running from, three adult hellhounds.

I started to move towards the portal, but Mason grabbed me. "You can't!" he yelled.

"He's in danger!" I said and struggled against him.

"That's his home and his life. We cannot interfere more than we already have. You cannot go in there and fight every hellhound to keep him safe."

"Run, pup! Run! Don't let them get you!"

The portal closed in front of us and I slid to my knees as I continued to watch the video. The pup continued to run, but the adults were gaining on him, getting closer and closer as their teeth snapped near his body.

"Lily, give me the phone," Mason said softly.

I shook my head. "I have to watch. I have to know what happens."

Something humanoid ran straight at him, but I couldn't see a face. The pup skid to a stop and yipped. Was that a *happy* yip?

The humanoid stayed just out of the camera's view and made a weird grunting sound before a hand wrapped around the phone and destroyed it, ending the video.

"You saw that, right?" I asked softly.

"He clearly knew that humanoid and seemed to think he was safe. So, I think we can assume he's safe now," Mason said.

Safe. I'd finally been able to save someone.

CHAPTER
TWENTY

"So," I said as Mason drove me back home, "are you going to tell everyone I harbored a demon pup?"

He huffed. "No, but only because you really were just trying to get it home and you thought of an idea that didn't require you to go through the portal to videotape it." He growled, "Even though you *did* try to run through the portal."

"Let's pretend that didn't happen," I said and flinched. Now that the pup was safe, I realized it had been a stupid idea to consider, but also ...

"I think you should tell everyone what happened, though."

"So, now that we know there are humanoids, are you guys going to try to go in?" I asked.

"We'll need to review the video and discuss it," he answered.

Assuming they weren't going to let me join in on that discussion, I asked, "Will you let me know what you decide?"

He frowned as he glanced at me before refocusing on the road again. "You don't want to participate?"

"I figured you wouldn't let me," I admitted. "You're the first one who's spoken to me since ..."

The silence was heavy as we drove through the gates and into our clan territory. He parked in the garage and turned to face me. "I'm still upset about it. I feel ... different and I don't know if it's a good different or not yet. I'm less angry in general, but that's not always a good thing, like when there's a fight. You took it from us without allowing us to have a say and it could have killed you and you would have just made us all watch. We had to sit there, blocked from getting to you, and watch as you exploded and possibly died. You have no idea what it was like to—"

"I watched my dad get killed, remember?" I whispered. "I do know. I also know from jumping in front of the spell meant for Mom." Thinking about it in those terms, I set a hand on his forearm and said, "I'm sorry. I was doing it to protect you all, to take back what you weren't supposed to have in the first place. You're right that I didn't take into account your feelings though, and all I can say is that I'm sorry."

He opened his mouth, but my door was pulled open and a very angry Kayden stood there. "What did you do?"

I blinked at the hostility. "What?"

"There's video of you sending a small hellhound through a portal. Please tell me it's fake," he said through gritted teeth.

Mason climbed out of the car and walked around to my side. "Let's take a breath, go inside, and we'll explain."

"You were with her?" Kayden growled. "I should have

known. You've always done whatever you could to keep her happy with you. The perfect lap dog."

Mason growled and stepped into Kayden's space, their faces inches apart. "That's rich coming from you. You stalked her so much I was counting down the days until you found a way to sneak a camera into her dorm."

"Fuck you. The only reason you weren't stalking her was because you were a kicked dog snarling from afar at your master."

"Because *I* didn't do anything. You're the one who fucked things up four years ago. Things were almost ruined because of you. Because you never think before you speak," Mason spat. "And you're about to do it again if you don't shut the fuck up and let us explain things."

"Boys, let's calm down," I said and stood out of the car, hands up placatingly. "We're all friends here, remember?"

"Are we? Because it seems that you've been keeping secrets not just from your family, but us, too," Kayden snapped.

"Everyone, inside!" Caleb roared from the house.

Flinching at the alpha order, we all speedwalked into the house, ducking our heads as we passed Dad and went into the living room.

"Start from the beginning," Mom said in a calm tone as she and my fathers sat across from us.

"Wait for me," Trey said as he stepped into the house and took a seat next to Tony on the smaller couch. "I'd like to hear this explanation as well."

Taking a deep breath, I said, "It all started with the necklace."

THREE HOURS LATER, I lay on the couch, talked out, and listened as my family and the trio discussed next steps.

"First things first, let's focus on the necklace," Mason said and looked at it on my chest.

My hand immediately went up to wrap around it. "It's a useful tool," I commented. "It helps us find the portals."

"Or, it's drawing them to you," Trey suggested.

"This was the first time we've had a portal open in our clan lands," Caleb pointed out.

Kayden quickly said, "We aren't saying you're drawing them, but the necklace, Lily."

My eyes narrowed because he'd known what I was thinking quickly.

"Try to take it off," Mason said.

Exhaling harshly through my nose, I reached back towards the clasp, but as my fingers neared it, my hands shook so much that I had to lower them and put them in my lap. Shaking my head, I said, "I can't."

"Can we try to remove it?" Mason asked and turned to face me. "Please?"

A hiss escaped before I could stop it and I slapped my hands over my mouth.

"So, this is our fault," Kayden whispered and his expression darkened. "We gave her that necklace knowing it came from a demon."

"We didn't know it came from the demon. We thought it had stolen it," Trey reminded him.

"We still knew it was demon related."

"That was kind of the point of the gift," Mason added.

"Boys!" Mom shouted. "Worry about your gift giving priorities later. Let's talk about this."

"I don't really want to fight her to try to remove it," Tony said and rubbed his ribs absentmindedly. "Last time we fought she wasn't even trying and bruised my ribs."

"Wait for her to fall asleep and try to remove it then?" Kayden said.

"You would suggest that, stalker," I hissed at him.

Everyone's eyes widened.

"Maybe we should talk about the necklace later," Tony said in a higher pitched voice than normal.

Scrubbing my face with my hands, I apologized, "Sorry."

"Why does my daughter think you're a stalker, Kayden?" Branson leaned forward on the couch menacingly.

"Can you pull up the video and screencast it to the TV?" Mason asked, distracting everyone.

Running upstairs, I grabbed my laptop, then ran back and hooked it up.

Everyone stared anxiously at the screen from when it started with him in the bag until the end when the humanoid had smashed the phone.

"Replay it at half speed," Riddick said.

We watched it a dozen more times.

"Send it to us so we can use enhancement software," Caleb ordered me.

"It's in our shared cloud server," I informed them.

They all looked over at me.

"You thought something was going to happen to you?" Mom guessed.

"Approaching demon portals is never safe," I whispered and looked down at my lap.

"You weren't scared of the demons," Mom whispered. "You were worried about the audience, weren't you?"

"That's why I was glad it was in the warehouse area, but apparently someone still videoed us." I sighed and leaned back on the couch, closing my eyes. "I try so hard to do things right, like I'm supposed to, but somehow they always get muddled up no matter how hard I try."

Mason set a hand on my leg and squeezed. "It's not the end of the world, Lily."

"I have a potential solution," Trey said.

"Let's hear it," Caleb replied.

I sat up and opened my eyes, eager to hear his suggestion.

"Everyone knows we're on special assignment to hunt demons. Everyone also knows that we've been friends with and recently started courting Lily. We can explain that this was her working with us, conducting an experiment, and share a single, image from the video." He held up his hand before anyone could comment. "Not an image of the humanoid or even the hounds, but one of the valley, minus the spire since that might incite panic. We already know the demons are coming from another place and this image will just give them that confirmation. Yes, it's going to open up the floodgates for them to want to know what our next steps are, and honestly, I think we should call a Summit to discuss it with everyone to make a determination. I definitely don't feel like my trio should make that decision."

"It is a good solution," Tony commented.

"Let's hold an emergency meeting with my parents to get their approval first," Caleb said. Looking at me, he said, "You're coming, too, cub."

"Okay," I agreed, feeling microscopically small.

Looking down, I realized Mason still had his hand on my leg.

A small smile formed, but I quickly stuffed it away. Now was not the time to gloat that he cared still.

"Mom? We have a situation. Where are my dads?" Caleb asked with his phone up to his ear.

"We should bring in the former royals, too," Mom suggested. "They've been dealing with the public and demon attacks longer than we've been alive."

Caleb nodded and continued talking to Nana Jolie.

"Are you hungry?" Mason asked.

"I am," I said. "I bet you are, too. I'll make something for everyone."

Standing, I hated the loss of his hand on my leg, his touch, but hurried to the kitchen to make something to eat.

Kayden followed me, but stayed a bit back, giving me some space. "I'm sorry," he whispered. "I shouldn't have yelled at you like that."

"No, you shouldn't have," I said and turned my back on him.

"I also shouldn't have ignored you the past couple of days." He sighed loudly. "I keep ruining things and I don't know how to stop. I'm just always worried about you, terrified that something bad is going to happen to you and I won't be there to protect you."

"You'll never be around me all the time," I said. "You have to learn to let me protect myself or accept that your brothers will keep me safe."

When he realized what I was making, he started pulling the other items necessary out to help me finish it. It was a simple enough dish, cook meat, add veggies, add water, simmer for fifteen minutes, add spices and herbs for the sauce, and let it stand so the sauce thickens. I made rice while it simmered, so it was ready in time to eat.

It was a common dish for us growing up because it could easily be doubled or tripled and kept for a week in the fridge.

"Oh, chicken curry!" Triston exclaimed as he walked into the kitchen. "I haven't had that in a while."

"Food's ready!" I called out and handed Triston a bowl. "Here, Tris."

He pecked me on the cheek. "You're the best daughter."

"I'm your only daughter," I said, but accepted the compliment all the same. I grabbed two bowls and filled them up for Mason and I. He'd started into the kitchen, but I held the bowl out for him. "Here. Thanks for helping me today and listening to me in the car."

Mason took the bowl and kissed my cheek. "You're welcome."

Trey stopped next to me, leaned over, and whispered in my ear, "You didn't text me about our next date, Princess."

"I was giving you time to deal with the changes from the extraction and decide how you wanted to proceed," I whispered back. "I was waiting for you to speak to me."

Straightening, he scowled. "Really?"

Feeling embarrassed, I nodded and headed to the dining table to eat my food. I sat beside Mason and my eyes widened at his already empty bowl. "Hungry, little fella?"

He stood and nodded. "Headed for seconds."

"Good thing I made a shifter sized batch," I chuckled.

Trey and Kayden sat across from me. Mom and Caleb sat at the ends of the table and everyone else filed in.

"Thank you for cooking, Lily and Kayden," Caleb said. "It's been a few years since we had curry last."

"I've been craving it," Mom sand and took a huge bite, moaning as she ate it. "So good!"

"Once we're done eating, we're going to meet everyone at my parents' house," Caleb said. "So, eat your fill because we're likely going to be there a while."

"Do I really have to go?" I asked softly.

"Yes, because you're the one with the demon handling experience," Trey said before my parents could speak.

"What was it like?" Mom asked.

"He reminded me of Tony," I said with a half-smile.

"How so?" Tony asked.

"He ate a butterfly after it landed on his nose, too."

Everyone laughed while Tony sighed.

"They understand our speech," I said. "I asked him to do a flip and he did one."

Everyone stared in shock at me.

"He felt like a hybrid shifter in a sense," I admitted. "Maybe he's a hybrid demon or something? I don't know, I just know that he wasn't trying to harm me, was scared of those bigger hounds, and listened to me. So, maybe our initial assumptions of the demons are all wrong. Maybe they aren't all evil, just like not all of us are good."

Their continued silent stares made me shift uncomfortably in my seat.

"I think you could be right," Mom said. "Though, we can't know for sure without more investigation. I did hear a voice that I thought was a random animal in the barn the past couple of days and it wasn't aggressive." She shrugged. "I can't know for sure if it was the pup, but the timing fits, so it could have been." One of Mom's powers was the ability to hear animal's thoughts and communicate with them. Once she communicated with them, it made them smarter, though, so she didn't do it often.

"I think it's probably a good thing you didn't let your mom talk to him. The last thing we need is smarter demons," Trey said.

That was something we could all agree on.

CHAPTER
TWENTY-ONE

The meeting turned into an overnight discussion that lasted through breakfast and finally ended at lunch.

Most of the time I was simply sitting in the background listening, but occasionally they would ask me questions about the pup and the demons I'd encountered.

They'd tried to remove the necklace in my sleep and I'd woken up coiled around Grandpa Foxfire who had apparently drawn the short straw.

"Okay, so we're in agreement, finally," Caleb said.

"Great!" I chirped. "I've got to run home and get ready for a date."

Mason and Kayden growled softly.

"Tell Prince Liam I said, 'hi,'" Grandpa Foxfire said.

Trey's eyes widened. "That's who you meant when you said, 'a couple princes?'"

"Mom, can you teleport me?" I requested, completely ignoring Trey's question.

"Wait, where's your calendar?" Kayden asked. "We haven't scheduled our second—"

"You didn't text her, so of course she hasn't responded," Mom interrupted. "Her calendar is at home, but since she's in a rush, you can message me and I'll find a date on the calendar for you." She waved and teleported me away.

"Dang, Mom. Just call 'em out in front of all the royals, why don't you?" Laughing, I shook my head and headed towards the stairs.

"They've got to prove themselves and part of proving themselves capable is being able to message and schedule events on their own." Mom shrugged. "It's part of being an adult, something they've been for several years now."

"Thanks for looking out for me," I said.

"Always," she promised. "And, while I am sad you didn't tell me about the pup, I do understand it. In your shoes, I probably would have done the exact same thing."

Giving her a big smile, I held back the tears that wanted to fall. "Thanks, Mom."

"Hurry! You're going to be late!" she shouted and shooed me to my room.

With record speed, I showered, changed, and drove to meet Liam at the address he'd given me.

I smiled as I parked at a theme park from a childhood show I used to love. My parents had brought me here several times because I'd begged them over and over again and demanded to do it at least twice for my birthday. Judging by the distinct lack of cars, he had rented the entire place out.

As soon as I climbed out of the car, I sighed, seeing

Kayden in fennec fox form, one he took only for spy missions, running from the back of my car and into the park. Some hybrids were blessed with more than one animal form, Kayden was able to transform into both a fennec fox and a white wolf.

I should have known one of them would demand to be my guard, but I had hoped my dads would veto them and come instead.

Deciding I would just ignore him and let him do his job of guarding me from actual threats, I headed towards the entrance where a burly werewolf named, Albert stood. "Hello, Albert," I greeted.

He bowed. "Hello, Princess Liliana. Prince Liam is waiting for you just inside."

"Thank you."

He leaned sideways, closer to me as I started by and whispered, "And I saw the pesky fox. We'll be sure to help keep him in hand."

Chuckling, I patted his shoulder. "I appreciate any help you can give me in that regard, Albert."

Through the turnstile, I was greeted with a park employee who held out a wristband. She smiled sweetly at me. "Good afternoon, Princess Liliana. Please let us know if you need anything."

I fastened the wristband and smiled. "Thank you for your work."

She snickered. "Working the park for two people is way better than thousands, so I should be thanking you. I get paid either way, but this is much easier."

"Glad I could be of service," I said and winked before

skipping through the arch that was the final entrance to the park.

Liam stood to the right, looking towards the entrance. When he saw me, he smiled and walked forward. "Hello, again."

"Hello, Liam. I have to say, I am very excited about this date. The last time I was here was over a decade ago."

"I thought it might be of interest to you. Though, I would have liked to keep it simpler, I did have to reserve the entire park or it would have been rather difficult for us to experience the rides."

"Completely understand," I said with a nod. "We'd become the main attraction if you hadn't rented it out."

He chuckled. "Exactly!" Holding out his bent elbow he asked, "Are you ready, milady?"

I slipped my arm through his and said, "Definitely!"

We nodded to an employee at the entrance to the nearest ride, a tall rollercoaster that went really fast and did a few loops. Once securely fastened to the ride, I smiled wide as it started.

"So, I saw the news," Liam commented as we moved up the first ramp. The clank-clank-clank of the pulleys moving us up the steep incline had my heart beating in excitement.

"Which news?" I asked, wanting to be sure I didn't give out information not public yet. I knew they would work fast, but wasn't sure if they had spread the cover story. Yes, Liam was a prince, but that didn't mean he was included in confidential discussions. Something I was fairly certain of since I was routinely involved in them.

"That you can control the demons and sent one back through the portal," he said.

"Ah, that's taken out of context," I said. "I don't control demons any more than I can control you."

He waited for me to elaborate.

Instead, I asked, "So, which is your favorite ride?"

"If we're going to be partners, you will have to share things with me," he said as the ride reached the crescendo right before the drop.

Before I could respond, the ride went down and I ignored him to enjoy the ride. Raising my arms over my head, I forgot that I was a twenty-five-year-old princess. I forgot I was courting several alpha males. I was just a person on a roller-coaster enjoying herself.

Smoothing my hair back as we pulled back into the entrance, I waited until we exited and were walking towards the next ride, away from any employees.

"Was this the real motivation to our courting? For you to try to gain 'insider royal knowledge' or something? I under-stand you're a prince who is left out of a lot of discussions and so you probably find it really unfair that I, as a princess who also won't take the throne, am involved in those discussions, but I don't make the decisions."

"What are you doing with those demons, Lily? Was that pup one sired by Mason with you?" he asked bluntly.

Fury boiled within me and before my mind thought better, I punched him in the face, knocking him flat on his back. "How dare you!" I snapped.

Really, what was it about me that two people thought I'd

sired the hellhound pup with someone? Was my pretty princess façade officially broken?

"I have not given birth to anything. And if it had been Mason's child, one, it wouldn't have been a hellhound, and two, I wouldn't have sent it away. Mason is twenty times the alpha you could hope to be." Laughing bitterly, I said, "I thought you were one of the good ones, but how quickly you showed your true colors. I suppose I should thank you for showing them so quickly. I'm leaving and I don't want to see you again."

He climbed to his feet, touching his broken nose. "So, the rumors of your anger issues are true. Good to know I dodged a bullet there. And that you do care about that insane psychopath."

Stepping up into his face, I said, "Say what you want about me, but stop badmouthing Mason."

"So, hybrids really will put out for anyone, huh? Good to know. I'll set my sights on your hybrid friend, Maya instead."

Why was he acting so differently than before? Was this really him?

"Are you under a spell? Possessed?" I asked. He hadn't lied when he'd said he'd had a crush on me in high school and thought this was an opportunity for him. Or had he phrased it in such a way to be able to pass my lie detection?

He rolled his eyes. "No, I'm just tired of pretending. That first date was torture. You really are a dull woman."

As I blinked in stunned silence at him, Kayden leapt from the nearby bushes, shifted, and punched Liam so hard that he spun in a corkscrew through the air and slammed head first into the fence ten feet away.

"Kay!" I gasped.

Several guards ran over to check on Liam and a few came towards us, but Kayden snarled at them.

Setting my hand on his arm, I asked, "How much did you hear?"

"Everything," he said tensely. Glancing at me, he said, "That was a nice punch you landed. Broke his nose perfectly."

A huge smile split my face. "One of the first fighting lessons Branson gave me was to punch rude boys in the face."

His mouth quirked. "I remember." He tapped his nose which had a bump on it. "That's how I got this."

I'd forgotten about that.

Brushing a finger down the bump I said, "I think it adds to your sexiness."

"Want to go ride the mountain ride?" he asked.

I glanced at the guards and the unconscious Liam. "Do you think we can?"

He arched a brow. "You're Princess Liliana of the Hybrids. You can do whatever you want. And I will destroy anyone who gets in your way."

Albert approached and Kayden tensed, but I stepped forward and said, "I'm sorry, Albert."

He shook his head. "We heard what he said. We wanted to intervene, but didn't want to get in trouble for butting into royal matters." He held out his fist and Kayden bumped his against it. "Thanks for doing what we all wanted."

Kayden smiled.

"We're going to go ride some more of the rides, okay?"

Albert nodded and gave us a big smile. "We'll escort the

prince out of the park, don't you worry. You may not be from my clan, but you are our king's favorite granddaughter, who I know would want you to have a great day and ignore this rude interruption."

Hugging him quickly I said, "Thank you, Albert."

Kayden waved for me to lead the way and once again, I found myself smiling wide and skipping through the park.

We got on my favorite ride in the park, one built like a mountain with a car that went through the mines, down a waterfall, and past a mythological monster called a yeti with glowing red eyes.

Gripping the rail, I screamed happily as we zoomed through the mountain ride, laughing and whooping with abandon.

Kayden joined me in laughing and whooping, which made me even happier. It was the first time I'd seen him let loose and enjoy himself really since we were in our early teens. Since before he got involved with the demons.

Grabbing his hand once we got off that ride, I dragged him as I ran to the next ride. We rode five more rides before I asked for water. There was a team of employees at the food vendor area, waiting expectantly for us. Their eyes did widen a bit when they saw Kayden instead of Liam, but they wisely made no comment.

We ordered our snacks and sat in the empty food court at a wooden table to eat.

"Oh, try this," I said and held out a bite of nacho cheese dipped pretzel.

He took the bite from my hand, his lips brushing my fingers as he took it. "Mm, that's as tasty as I remember."

We spent the next twenty minutes feeding each other bites of food while laughing and teasing each other as the sun set.

It was the perfect end to what could have been an awful night.

Walking to the parking lot, I whispered, "I feel like the three of you are always saving me."

"Well, that's kind of our job," he said and shrugged.

"I'm a job to you?" I asked, smirking.

His head whipped around to look at me, mouth open, but his mouth closed when he saw my teasing expression. "Brat."

Looping my arm around his waist, I pulled him to a stop and hugged him. "Thank you."

He hugged me back and rested his head atop mine. "You're welcome."

We stood like that for several minutes before releasing each other and getting in the car and heading home.

CHAPTER
TWENTY-TWO

"What a scumbag!" Maya shouted as we drank our first drinks in a VIP section of a different club. I didn't want to go to Great Uncle Gavin's club again and risk the trio showing up. She'd insisted on going out after I had told her what happened with Liam and I had agreed as long as we brought two guards for protection. The last thing I wanted was Liam to find us and start drama.

The trio had tried to join us, but I'd convinced Riddick and Triston to be our guards instead after explaining I wasn't coming to find anyone to dance with, but to just enjoy myself and dance with Maya.

"Yeah, I'm glad he showed what he was really like early, though." I couldn't imagine what could have happened if I had turned down the trio, accepted Liam, and found out what a complete douche he was.

"Let's go dance. I need to burn off this rage," Maya growled and stomped towards the rope to enter the dance area.

With my dads nearby, people thankfully steered clear of us, allowing us to enjoy our time without interruption. We returned to our booth and caught our breath while also enjoying more drinks.

"This was just what I needed, thanks, girl." I said and clinked my glass against hers.

She smiled wide. "That's what besties are for! So, as your bestie, can I just say that I don't understand your hesitation. Like ... at all."

"Hesitation for what?" I asked, frowning.

"To finalize your promise, to take the guys as your mates. You and the trio have been ideal partners since they were born. Seriously, it was like Ezio had a child to fulfill a prophecy of being your mate or something. It's just meant to be. Why the hesitation?"

"It's not that simple," I whispered.

She arched a brow. "It is. They've been in love with you for decades. And you've been in love with them for decades."

"That power I shared with them could have been altering their true feelings," I said.

"And yet, even with the power back inside of you, and them still obviously all about you, you're hesitating. Kayden punched a prince for you and then rode rollercoasters to ensure you had a good day. Mason helped you send a demon back through a portal because you asked him to. Trey snuffs any female who so much as looks at him. He also monitors social media and destroys anyone who talks negatively about you."

"I'm sorry, he does what?" This was the first I'd heard of it.

She nodded. "He made me swear not to tell you, but I think you need to know. They do all kinds of things behind the scenes." She giggled. "That rhymed!"

"So, what you're telling me, is that even while I had blocked them, they were still protecting me and doing things to help me?"

She nodded again. "Yep." She made the p sound pop extra loud.

"What if the power—"

Groaning, she flopped backwards in the booth and flailed around on the couch. "Stop it! You're a freaking goddess and deserve loyal men who can protect you. Those men are undoubtedly loyal and of the men our age, the most likely capable of protecting you. They know the drawbacks and issues of being with a royal and a hybrid and they don't care. Stop being a pain and accept it already!"

I blinked at her for a few seconds before bursting into laughter, tears trickling down my face. "I ... never thought ... you would be ... telling me ... to accept them as mates."

"Me neither! Yet, here we are!" Her cheeks puffed and were pink in her exasperation.

Hugging her, I said, "You're the bestest best friend ever."

"Duh," she replied in a super sarcastic tone.

"Instead of dancing more, why don't we head home for ice cream and comedy shows? I saw a new comedy special available."

Her eyes brightened, she leapt to her feet, and said, "You had me at ice cream."

Raising my hand, I waved for my dads even though I couldn't see exactly where they were. I could find them by their auras if I wanted to, but I just waited instead. Triston and Riddick stepped out of the shadows behind our booth.

"Ready to go home?" Triston asked with a wide smile. He was always smiling and happy. Like I tried to be.

Riddick stood with a serious expression, like he almost always was. His smiles were rare and awesome.

"Yes," I said with a nod.

"Do we need to stop for snack supplies?" Riddick asked.

"Yes," Maya said and nodded emphatically.

"We don't need snacks. We have everything at home," I told her and shook my head. "Have you forgotten who I live with? There's always an abundance of snacks."

"Oh, right," she said.

Exiting the club, we were blinded by camera flashes and deafened by shouted questions and names being called.

"Princess! Is it true you're assisting with the demon research?" someone yelled.

"Is it true that you've been courting mates and rejected Prince Liam?" another asked.

The urge to answer that question was strong, but Riddick stepped between the person and I and said, "No comments at this time."

How did they find out about Liam already?

Triston opened the door for us with a flourish. "Ladies."

The drive home was uneventful, but full of Triston and Maya gossiping, which gave me time to think about what she'd said.

The trio were always there for me and the misunderstanding had been partially my fault. I had been harboring feelings for them since I was a teenager. I'd hidden it when we were in high school as much as I could, but it was so much harder now.

And maybe Maya was right. Maybe I needed to stop acting like the main character in a novel and just admit my feelings to them.

Choosing your mates was a huge deal and not done lightly. So, perhaps it was time to at least take the next step and court them exclusively.

That would give them time to confirm that they did love me, without the power, and to confirm we were ideal mates.

Walking into the house, laughing and smiling, we headed straight for the kitchen.

"Where is everyone?" Riddick asked.

I paused in taking the ice cream out of the freezer and listened. There were no other sounds aside from the ones we were making. "Did they message you?"

Maya grabbed a bowl and started scooping out her ice cream. "They're probably dealing with the blowout from Liam or something. There's always some issue for the royals to handle."

Riddick tried to call someone, but they obviously didn't answer by the growl he released and the immediate next dial.

Triston tried to call someone next.

Heading to the TV, I turned it on to the local news station, hoping my gut feeling was wrong.

"A giant portal has opened in the center of the downtown park," the newscaster declared.

"Well, I found them," I announced loud enough for Riddick, Triston, and Maya to hear.

They all ran into the living room to look at the TV where

most of my family and the trio were being videoed at the scene.

"Let's go," Riddick growled.

"Let me throw on sweats!" I shouted and ran up the stairs, changing as quickly as I could and grabbing a pair for Maya to change into in the car.

Riddick drove, being the better driver of the four of us, but that also gave Maya time to change and me time to put my hair up and slip on socks and tennis shoes.

"I'm glad we're the same size," Maya commented as she put on the tank top that I had given her.

"Very convenient for times like this," I agreed with a nod.

Due to so many people in the streets, we had to park and run the rest of the way.

As we approached, Mason, Kayden, and Trey spun around, eyes fixed on me, like that had sensed my approach.

"What's the status?" I asked.

"Your necklace reacting?" Trey asked.

Eyes widening, I realized that it wasn't warm like usual. "No," I admitted and shook my head.

That had them all scowling.

Staring up at the giant portal, I had an uneasy feeling, like something crazy was about to happen. The darkness within me stirred. We were lucky that the park had a lot of lights, so it was easy to see if anything came out.

Mom walked over from where she had been gathered talking to Branson, Caleb, and my grandads. "Sorry we didn't call."

Triston brushed a kiss across her cheek. "Apology accepted." He walked by her and hurried over to Caleb.

"What's the status?" Riddick asked.

"Nothing has come out so far," Trey answered. "It appeared twenty minutes ago."

"Oh, they answer him," I muttered to Maya out of the side of my mouth who laughed softly.

"You ever seen a portal this large before?" Riddick asked.

"No," all three answered simultaneously.

Riddick sighed and rubbed a hand down his face. "That's what I feared." Heading away from us, he walked over to confer with the rest of my family.

"I'm going to see if I can hear what they're saying to snoop a bit," Maya said and walked slowly towards the group.

Trey turned to me and said, "Kayden told us what happened with Liam."

Frowning, I rubbed my left arm with my right hand. "Oh."

"Don't worry, I've got my social media team ensuring he doesn't post anything on his account or a fake account to lie about the incident," Trey said.

"I appreciate that, but it's really not necessary."

He frowned down at me. "I disagree. It is one hundred percent necessary."

"I think we should pay him a visit to teach him what happens to misbehaving royals," Mason said and cracked his knuckles.

"Kayden and I already punched him," I reminded them, but couldn't hide the smile that spread. "I appreciate you three looking out for me."

"Lily!" Mom called.

"We better meet up with them," I said. "After, I'd like to talk to you guys, okay?"

Their eyes widened and they looked at each other.

Jogging over, I was immediately hugged by Grandpa Foxfire. "I'm so sorry about that rude elf! He's already gotten an earful from both me and Mom and it's not the last of it. To be so disrespectful is outrageous for any man, not to mention a prince." He kissed my head. "My poor granddaughter."

Laughing, I patted his back. "Thanks, Grandpa, but I'm okay. Kayden punching him and finishing the day going on rides with me helped."

"We're going to split up into two teams," Caleb explained. "One on each side of the portal to ensure we see anything that comes out."

"Okay," I said with a nod.

Caleb pointed as he split up the teams, "Mas, Trey, Ember, Deryn, Rhys, and Lily will stay on this side. Jolie, Kay, Foxfire, Nico, Maya, and I will go to the far side."

Kayden didn't like being separated, but he didn't argue. He did stop next to me and whisper, "Don't do anything reckless."

I saluted him extra sarcastically, "Yes, sir!"

Rolling his eyes, he kissed me on the cheek before jogging after Caleb.

Mom waved to get our attention. "Let's spread out, that way we're ready if something does come out. We want to ensure whatever comes out doesn't escape into the city or harm the civilians."

Mason walked next to me with his sword already drawn. "If your necklace starts warming up, alert us, okay?"

I nodded.

He set a hand on my arm, leaned over, and rubbed his cheek along mine. He had stubble along his jaw from not shaving for several days, but it was thankfully long enough to be soft instead of poky. "I'll stay as close as I can."

"Protecting the civilians is more important," I whispered and breathed in his scent, drawing it in like it was my first breath after being submerged.

"How many times do I have to tell you that you're the most important being in the world to me?" He kissed my lips and winked. "I'll show you later, if you let me."

Swallowing hard, I hissed, "Tease."

Chuckling, he jogged away from me, trying to space himself as the others spread out, too.

"You okay?" Trey asked. "Any feelings of wanting to run through the portal?"

"No," I sighed loudly. "You want me to back up ten more feet than you guys are so you'll know if I get an urge?"

He pinched my cheek before kissing the sting away. "Yes, please."

"Oh, I like it when you say please. You should do it more often." I backed up, giving him the ten feet even though I'd been joking when I'd said it.

He winked. "Praise kink noted."

My cheeks were suddenly an inferno.

Mom smiled knowingly at me, but after a second of eye contact, everyone focused on the task at hand.

Watching the giant demon portal for anything coming out.

"Mas and Rhys, watch top," Mom ordered. "Trey and Deryn, watch mid. Deryn and Lily, watch bottom."

"Okay," we all agreed verbally to let her know we'd heard.

There were tons of onlookers, people gathering in the streets beyond to watch and see what might happen. Thankfully, there were a lot of alphas keeping them back and also adding to our numbers if something did happen.

Ezio was among them and even had Holly at his side. I also saw Kieran among the crowd with Sheila.

Was the entire city here?

An hour of standing later, I squatted and stood, flexing my legs to keep them warm in preparation of fighting.

The necklace warmed against my chest.

"Necklace!" I yelled. Immediately after, five bull-headed demons stepped out of the portal.

"Bottom!" Deryn and I yelled simultaneously.

Unfortunately, our call was echoed from the opposite side of the portal as well.

"Coming out of both sides? Has that happened before?" I asked Trey who moved closer to me.

He shook his head. "Never."

"Top!" Mason yelled on our side at the same time Maya yelled it from the other side.

Two large bird-like demons with huge beaks and feathers that looked like they were made from the same spikes that the hellhounds had flew out of the portal and circled us.

"My turn to hunt," Trey said, winked, shifted into his dragon form, and took to the sky.

My heart beat faster as I watched him head to fight the bird-demons and Mason fight against the bull-demons.

Moving closer to Mom in the center, I clutched at the necklace as it grew even hotter.

"I've got a bad feeling, Mom," I whispered.

"It's alright, Lily. We're all here together," she whispered as she used her telekinesis to grab rocks from the ground and fling them at the bull-demons, hitting them in the head and making them stumble to give Mason and Deryn an advantage as they fought them.

Since I'd moved closer to the middle, I wasn't able to see around the portal to know how the other side was doing. I had to trust in my family and friends and their strength.

Surrounding this portal were the most powerful people in the entire world. If we couldn't defeat the creatures, there was no hope for the rest of the world.

From the bottom of the portal ran a familiar hellhound pup with the cord from the cellphone bag around his neck still. He looked larger, like he'd grown at least three months older when it had only been a day since we'd sent him back. He ran out, looked around, saw me, and his tongue lulled out of the side of his mouth as he barked and ran at me.

"Don't kill him!" I shouted.

Mom's eyes widened as she watched the hellhound run at me. "He knows you. He's yelling about being here to protect you."

"What?" I gasped, looking at her.

She nodded. "He just keeps repeating, 'Protect Princess. Protect Princess,' over and over again."

But why? Was he here on his own or had the humanoid sent him?

Six giant humanoid bodied demons with pig-like heads, thick arms and legs, and large curved tusks walked out of the portal carrying large wooden clubs.

The hellhound made it to me and jumped around me in a circle, yipping happily.

"Hello, pup," I greeted. "Are you here to protect me?"

He barked, turned, spread his legs, and growled. The quills along his body spread and vibrated, making a sound similar to a rattlesnake's rattle. He looked back at me, his tongue rolled out of the side of his mouth, and snorted. Clearly proud of himself.

"Stay next to me," I ordered him. "I don't want those big hellhounds picking on you again."

He snorted again and rolled his eyes.

"He said, 'they won't come near me this time. They were punished,'" Mom translated.

She and I exchanged a look before focusing back on the battle.

The bull-demons and bird-demons were dead, so Trey, Mason, Grandpa Rhys, and Grandpa Deryn were focused on the giant pig-demons now.

I felt useless, but knew in battles like this it was important to have someone to call out new enemies and provide backup.

The pup turned towards the portal and growled low and menacing.

Four hellhounds, much larger than any hellhound I'd seen before, ran out of the portal and headed straight for Mom and I.

Was it a trap? Was the pup just a ruse and he would turn and attack us?

Taking a warrior form, I prepared to launch myself at the hellhounds to keep them away from Mom.

Mom yanked two large boulders from the ground and threw them at the hellhounds. It hit one in the face, but the other three dodged them.

The pup stepped forward, growling and puffed up, his quills rattling. As the hellhounds got closer, he darted forward and clacked his teeth together. Pacing back and forth in front of Mom and I, he made a snarling, snapping, quill rattling wall.

The hellhounds skidded to a stop before they reached him, growling with spit flying from their snouts, but after one last look at us, they turned and headed towards the others.

"Well, I'll be a rabbit's auntie," Mom whispered.

CHAPTER
TWENTY-THREE

The pup trotted back to me and sat on his rump at my side.

Reaching down, I patted the top of his head, being careful of the direction of his quills. "Good boy."

The ground shook beneath our feet, making all of us gasp.

As it continued to shake, I realized it was footsteps.

"Giant!" I shouted just as the largest demon we had ever seen stepped out of the portal; its head reached almost the top of the portal. It was covered in thick, shaggy, purple fur, had two horns curving down around his face, and a face that looked like a warrior shifted werewolf.

"Is that a werewolf demon?" Mom asked softly.

The pup tilted his head back and howled. All the remaining hellhounds joined the howl.

Wolf howls had always been calls of friends and family, something happy to me, but in this moment, the hair on my nape rose and I felt fear shudder through me.

The giant werewolf-demon lowered his head, looked at everyone, and focused on Mom and I, though I had an awful feeling it was me he was really focused on.

"Mom," I whispered and swallowed hard, "I think it's me."

"I see that, Lily." She created a portal beneath my feet and I fell through to the other side, right next to Caleb.

"Giant werewolf-demon!" I shouted at him as I gasped for breath since I'd not been prepared for the portal Mom had created and fallen onto my back. "After me, we think."

Caleb was in a warrior form that combined all of his heritage of dragon, werewolf, mage, elf, and siren. We called it his ultimate form. His eyes glowed silver as he snarled and said, "No one touches my daughter."

The giant werewolf-demon stepped around the portal, each step making the ground shake, and continued until he saw me.

"Yep, definitely after you," Kayden said, suddenly behind me.

Tony ran from the other side of the portal.

"About time you showed up," I grumbled at him.

"I was on the other side of town. Mom told me to come stay near you."

"That's after her," Kayden said and pointed at the giant werewolf-demon.

Tony sighed. "Of course it is. Why wouldn't Mom have sent me to do an easier job?"

"Keeping Lily safe has never been an easy job," Kayden muttered.

"Hey!" I snapped at them and put my hands on my hips. "I've been fine for years without you by my side. Don't even start."

The pup ran around from the opposite side and I screamed once again, "Don't kill the pup!"

Foxfire spun in a circle to keep the sword he'd begun to strike the pup with away.

The pup ran to me, whined, and sat beside me.

"Mom said he's here to protect me. He sent four hell-hounds away from Mom and I, so we believe him."

Kayden's lip twitched as he looked at the pup, but he didn't comment.

Tony just sighed and shook his head again.

Caleb ran at the giant werewolf-demon, sent a bolt of electricity at it, and ran for its legs as it howled in pain.

"Maybe you should help Dad?" I suggested to Tony.

He looked at me and then at the giant werewolf-demon. "Helping to take that down would help protect you."

"Go," I urged. "I'd rather you help keep Dad safe."

He looked at Kayden and said, "Don't let her out of your sight."

Kayden bumped fists with him and Tony ran to help Dad.

Nana Jolie squatted by the pup and smiled. "Hello, pup! You're adorable!"

The pup yipped and let his tongue lull out of his mouth again, wagging his tail so fast it raised a small dust cloud.

My laughter was short-lived as the giant werewolf-demon was taken to his knees by Caleb, Grandpa Nico, Tony and

Grandpa Foxfire. The giant werewolf-demon tilted his head back and made an incredibly eerie howl that had everyone taking a step back and all of the shifters, myself included, growling or hissing.

The necklace warmed against my chest again. "Kay, the necklace," I whispered.

Nana Jolie and he looked at the necklace, brows furrowing.

The next instant, four extremely humanoid demons stepped out of the portal. They had pale skin, long horns atop their heads pointed up and curving slightly backwards, short thick light brown hair, hooved feet, and had extremely muscular bodies, even more muscular than the shapeshifters currently fighting for their lives. They didn't have any weapons, which worried me. When someone didn't carry a weapon to a battle, it was normally because they considered their bodies the only weapons they needed. My worry tripled when they started running and their long strides were incredibly fluid.

Kayden stepped forward, growling in his werewolf warrior form. "Move back," he ordered us.

Nana Jolie shifted into her warrior form, drawing on the connection between her four mates and her, and stepped between Kayden and I. She glanced at the hellhound pup and said, "You better protect her, pup."

The pup bobbed his head once and got to his feet, puffing up and rattling his spines.

Maya noticed that Kayden was about to face off against four strong-looking demons on his own, squawked to get Grandpa Foxfire's attention, and flew towards us.

Kayden slammed into the first demon and their battle was incredibly intense, so much so that my eyes were locked on them and didn't pay attention to the three remaining ones who charged straight towards me.

"Mas!" Kayden bellowed as he exchanged blows with the humanoid demon.

Nana Jolie and Grandpa Foxfire each attacked one of the humanoids and Maya began to fling fire at the last one.

Jumping forward, I began attacking the one Maya was hitting with fire as well, both of us used to coordinating our attacks since it was something we'd practiced for hundreds, possibly thousands, of hours growing up.

The pup whined and paced behind me, but strangely did not help attack the humanoid demon. Was it because it was so much more powerful than him?

The humanoid demon grabbed a rock from the ground and threw it at Maya, hitting her and causing her to fall to the ground.

"Maya!" I screamed and ran towards her.

The humanoid demon grabbed me around the waist, flung me over his shoulder, and started running towards the portal.

Mason slammed into the humanoid demon in his human form, knocking us to the ground. I shifted into my full snake form and wrapped around the demon, constricting tighter and tighter as I coiled my body around him.

"You okay?" Mason asked as he stood beside me, looking around our side of the portal's battle scene.

As if I could speak to him in my snake form while constricting.

The humanoid demon fighting Kayden hit him so hard that he flew at least forty feet away. Free from Kayden's attacks, he ran at us.

Mason shifted his feet into his raven talons and with a slashing kick, cut into the demon's chest.

The demon gasped and jumped forward, tackling Mason to the ground and wrestling with him.

The humanoid demon I was trying to kill was surprisingly still alive, still breathing, and none of his bones had broken even though I was using all of my strength.

Glancing over, I hissed at finding Nana Jolie on the ground and Foxfire losing his battle.

The humanoid demon fighting Mason had him on the ground, hands around his throat.

We were losing. This wasn't good.

What could I do?

I shifted my head so I could speak. "What do you want?" I hissed at the humanoid I was coiled around.

He blinked then in very slow words said, "You. Princess."

"Me?" I asked.

He nodded.

"If I go, you'll all leave?" I asked.

He nodded again.

"Prove it," I said, shifted to my human form, and stepped back from him. He stood, and brushed himself off, then waved towards the portal.

The demon who had been choking Mason let up enough to just keep him pinned.

Looking down at Mason I said, "Remember that second

part of our promise? To always protect each other? That's what I'm doing."

He tried to shift to break free of the demon, but it continued to use its superior strength to hold him.

As I walked towards the portal, I caught Caleb's eye as he continued to battle the giant werewolf-demon. He was about to defeat it. I just needed to stall long enough for them to get free to fight these humanoids.

I did not want to go through that portal. No matter how curious I was about what was on the other side and the strange pull I felt.

The rage and power within me were non-responsive. It felt like the necklace was pulsing against my chest, but I couldn't even raise my hands to try to remove it.

The pup trotted next to me, happy and prancing. Did he know they were going to take me?

One humanoid demon walked in front of me while the other walked behind me.

The giant werewolf-demon fell, officially dead, freeing Caleb and Grandpa Nico turned, focused now on the newest threats.

Just as they moved towards me, a dozen similar humanoid demons ran out to create a wall around us.

Shit.

I tried to run towards them, but the humanoid demon who had been behind me, grabbed me around the waist, pressed his fingers against my neck, and I immediately became paralyzed.

My body went completely limp and no matter what I

tried, I couldn't move. My power remained locked and unusable.

"Dad!" I screamed, my voice somehow working despite the spell.

"Lily!" Caleb, Grandpa Nico, and Mason screamed.

Mom ran around the corner, created a portal beneath the feet of the demon carrying me, to try to send us away, but the demon in front of us grabbed his partner and pulled him away from the portal before we fell. "Give me my daughter!" Mom screamed.

Time seemed to move in slow motion as the demon carrying me ran towards the portal and all of my family tried to battle through the demons to get to me.

Mom and Grandpa Nico teleported right next to me, using spells to incapacitate the demons stealing me.

I fell out of the demon's arms and rolled on the ground.

Mom stepped over me, created a stone box around us, and said, "I've got you, Lily."

"Can't move my body," I whispered.

It was too dark in the box to see her expression.

"We'll heal whatever's been done to you. Kara and I will do whatever we can to fix it."

I believed her, too. They were the best healers in the world.

A voice, one that sounded vaguely familiar whispered in my mind, *"We won't hurt you. Just accept your destiny."*

My destiny? What did that mean?

"Accept your destiny, Goddess."

The title made me realize it was the same voice as the one

who had told me to accept the shadow power to become a goddess. What did all this mean?

"*It means, you have to come to us.*"

Us?

Something smashed into the stone box we were in, completely shattering it and sending Mom flying through the air.

A large male demon wearing battle armor and a helmet that covered his face towered over me, a silver, spiked mace in his hand. He emitted an immense power and alpha aura.

"What do you want?" Caleb demanded as everyone froze, afraid to move with him right over my prone body.

"All will be revealed in good time," the demon said.

"I love you!" I shouted at my family, friends, and the trio. They might not realize those words were for them, but they were.

Closing my eyes, I prepared for the demon to kill me, to crush my head with the mace.

There was a chaos of movement, growls, battle cries, and roars. It was so loud it blended together in a cacophony of insanity.

The necklace warmed against my chest, so much warmer than had ever happened before.

And then ...

Silence.

I opened my eyes and stared at the unfamiliar landscape of burned grasslands and trees before me. A spire in the distance caught my eye and I realized it wasn't so unfamiliar ... it was the demon world.

I was in the demon world.

FIND out what happens next in Their World (Her Royal Harem: Lily #2) catbanks.co/Lily

ABOUT THE AUTHOR

Catherine Banks is an award-winning, USA Today bestselling author who writes in several romance subgenres and has multiple pseudonyms. She began writing fiction at only four years old and finished her first full-length novel at the age of fifteen. She is married to her soulmate and best friend, Avery, who she has two amazing children with. After her full-time job, she reads books, plays video games, and watches anime shows and movies with her family to relax. Although she has lived in Northern California her entire life, she dreams of traveling around the world. Catherine is also C.E.O. of Turbo Kitten Industries™, a company with many hats including being a book publisher and store full of nerdy fun.

facebook.com/catherinebanksauthor
bookbub.com/authors/catherine-banks
amazon.com/author/catherinebanks

CONNECT WITH CATHERINE BANKS

I really appreciate you reading my book! Here are some ways to connect with me:
www.catherinebanks.com

Join my newsletter for deals and snippets:
http://catbanks.co/newsletter